ALBUQUERQUE ACADEMY

1955

This book was donated
to honor
the birthday of

Kevin Lewis '97

by

Kathy Lewis Lepley

January 3, 1991

DATE

KING
TUT'S
GAME
BOARD

KING TUT'S GAME BOARD

LEONA ELLERBY

LERNER PUBLICATIONS COMPANY
MINNEAPOLIS

King Tut's Game Board was designed and illustrated by Susan Hopp. The text was set in 11½-point Edelweiss, with titles and headings in Koronna Bold and Extra Bold. The oval figure, or cartouche, that appears at the beginning of each chapter is a hieroglyphic rendering of "Nebkheperura," the name taken by Tutankhamon when he became pharaoh. Additional information about Tutankhamon and the other pharaohs of Egypt can be found in the historical charts that appear at the end of the book.

International Standard Book Number: 0-8225-0765-X
Library of Congress Catalog Card Number: 79-91279

2 3 4 5 6 7 8 9 10 90 89 88 87 86 85 84 83 82 81

To Bill, for his encouragement
To Carol, Hap, and Billy, for their enthusiasm
To Justin, my inspiration

KING TUT'S GAME BOARD

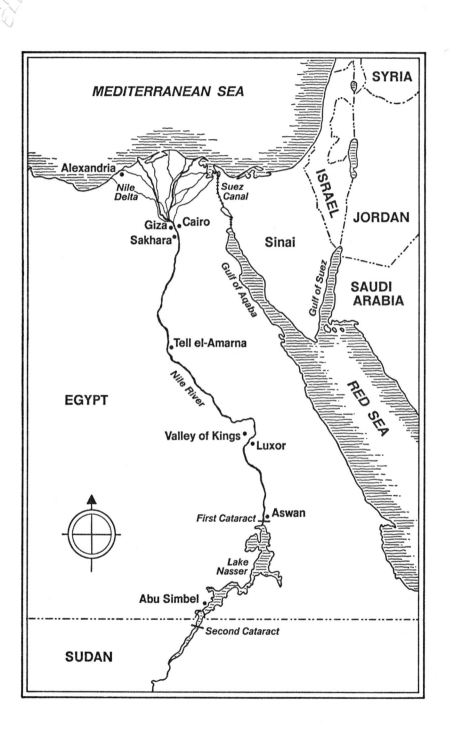

CHAPTER
1

JUSTIN SANDERS' NOSE WAS PRESSED AGAINST THE TINY window of the jet as it slowly taxied to a stop at the Cairo airport. When the doors of the 707 opened, Justin and the other passengers gasped for breath. Hot, dusty, strange-smelling air surrounded them as they prepared to leave the plane. Beyond the airfield, where the horizon met the clear sky, they could see a desert sunset in progress.

In the international passenger lounge, fans dried the perspiration already formed on their faces. Justin put down his flight bag and looked around at the large posters showing the pyramids, the Great Sphinx, and other Egyptian antiquities, which covered the walls of the room.

"Have your passport ready," Justin's father, Jud Sanders, said, "and for heaven's sake keep your health certificate handy too. It won't be long, and we'll be out of here."

After waiting in line for a short time, Mr. Sanders and his wife, Miriam, approached the desk of the customs official, with Justin trailing behind them.

"Why are you visiting Egypt?" the official asked.

"For purely recreational reasons," Mr. Sanders replied.

The answer seemed to satisfy the official, and the Sanders were hurried through customs with no more delay. Their passports were stamped, and they were released once again into the oppressive heat. Leaving the airport, they were met by a throng of porters and taxi drivers. Mr. Sanders hired a vintage 1942 Fiat to take them to their hotel.

"Damn, it's hot!" said Mr. Sanders, taking off his coat before getting into the taxi.

"Soon comes the breeze off the river, sir," said the driver cheerfully. "You'll see, in just one hour." Amazingly, he was wearing a jacket and showed no sign of being aware that it was a miserably hot evening.

Pulling out into the traffic around the airport, the driver smiled in the rear view mirror at his three tired, uncomfortable passengers. "It's good to have you British back. Welcome to Egypt." The taxi driver was recalling the old days in Cairo when the British were everywhere, but Mr. Sanders was not amused by his mistake.

"We're Americans," he said indignantly, and a little pompously.

The driver made no reply, giving all his attention to maneuvering the cab through the heavy traffic. Soon they entered the central area of the crowded, noisy city. Everywhere the Sanders could see policemen in white uniforms and black berets trying to create order out of the chaos of cars, carts, bicycles, and pedestrians that filled the streets.

After a ride that Justin thought would never end, they tumbled gratefully out of the taxi in front of the majestic Nile

Hilton Hotel. Just then, a breeze ruffled their hair.

"See," said the driver, "I told you. One hour, and the breeze comes up, like magic." He seemed to feel personally responsible for this cool breath of air.

After checking in, Mr. Sanders gave the room keys to his son while he and his wife went into the dark, cool comfort of the cocktail lounge to have a drink. Justin helped a porter to carry the six pieces of luggage up to the suite he would share with his parents. The porter seemed impressed by Justin's slow but flawless Arabic and by the 25-piaster tip that he received. After he left, Justin started sizing up what would be his home for the next three weeks. He would rather have stayed at a small hotel run by local people, but he was so grateful just to be here that he wouldn't complain about the luxurious, plastic surroundings offered by the Hilton.

By the time his parents made it up to their room, Justin had unpacked his clothes, checked the television, taken the paper off the toilet seat, used one of the water glasses, and read a pamphlet about night life in Cairo. He was waiting, restlessly, for their appearance.

"I'm starved!" he said as they entered the room. "Do you mind if I pick up a sandwich downstairs instead of eating with you? Later I'd like to try out the pool. I'll be back around ten. Okay?"

Miriam Sanders was secretly thankful to hear Justin's plans for the evening. For her, vacation time meant elegant, leisurely meals prepared and served by someone else, and dressing up to enjoy them. Tonight, mellowed by the cocktail she'd just had, she wanted to dine alone with her husband. Before he could object, she said, "That's fine, Justin. This is your vacation too, and you should do what you want." She glanced at her husband and added, "Within reason, of course."

Mr. Sanders grunted. "Be careful," he said over his shoulder as he went to the bathroom to take a shower.

Justin had one of the room keys already pinned to his swim trunks under his jeans and a towel over his arm. He hurried out of the room and headed for the stairs rather than waiting for the elevator. They were on the sixth floor, and walking down would be welcome exercise after a day of traveling.

In the lobby he stopped to study a map of the hotel and its grounds. He discovered that there was an outdoor dining area next to the pool. Great! That's where he'd eat tonight.

He went out the double doors, which were closed to keep the lobby cool, and looked casually around for a place to sit. It seemed everybody had the same idea he did. There wasn't an unoccupied table to be seen. Justin fervently hoped he wouldn't have to wait too long; he could already feel his empty stomach protesting. As his eyes became accustomed to the dark, relieved only by the lights in the pool and the small lanterns on the tables, he spotted a boy sitting alone at a table for four. His hunger overcame his usual reluctance to impose on others—especially others his own age. He ambled coolly (he hoped) over to the table, which was right next to the pool.

"Hi!" he said. "Are you waiting for someone else? Do you mind if I sit down here?"

The boy looked up at Justin. He seemed startled and unsure of himself as he mumbled something: his father might come— but then again, he might not—and he guessed it was all right because there would still be room for him if he did come...

Justin was already regretting his impulsiveness. His dad was right. He was a loner, and even strangers didn't want his company. His appetite fled as his nervousness increased.

"Never mind. I'll wait for another table," he muttered as he started to back away.

"No. No. Please sit down." The boy jumped to his feet, finally remembering his manners. "It's just that this is the first

time someone, uh, someone like you has, uh, wanted to..."
His dark complexion turned darker with embarrassment.

Justin recognized the boy's discomfort and quickly forgot his own feelings of rejection.

"Thanks. Thanks a lot. I haven't eaten forever, it seems, and I just couldn't wait any longer."

He pulled out a chair and sat down.

"How's the food here? What do you recommend? Is that sandwich you're eating any good?" Justin rattled on and on, unable to stop the inanities pouring off his tongue.

"My name's Justin Sanders," he continued, "and I've only just arrived. I'm here with my folks. They're eating in the hotel dining room. I couldn't wait for them 'cause my mom takes forever to get dressed. We live in Saudi Arabia. In Jidda. My dad works for a big oil company and I go to an American school there. This is my first trip to Cairo even though we've lived in the Middle East for almost three years now."

My God, he thought, won't somebody please make me shut up! In another five minutes, he'll have my whole life history.

The boy leaned over the table and shook Justin's hand. Justin was startled at this formality. The only times he'd shaken hands with kids his own age had been after a tennis match or a soccer game.

"I'm very pleased to make your acquaintance, Justin. My name is Nathan Alistant, but my family calls me Nate. I don't like the food here, but it is tolerable. I recommend the sliced beef sandwich—that's what I'm eating."

He had answered all of Justin's questions in careful, correct English and in the same stacatto manner that Justin had asked them. After Nate had spoken, both boys settled into an uncomfortable silence that was finally broken by the waiter coming over to take Justin's order.

Justin took this opportunity to impress the formal young

man across the table by ordering the sandwich Nate had recommended in Arabic. The surprised waiter beamed his appreciation at Justin and said, "Just like your young friend." He gestured towards Nate. "You, too, have mastered our language."

Justin looked at Nate and saw him smiling. The strangeness between the boys was starting to dissolve with the realization that they had at least this one thing in common.

Justin's appetite had completely returned by the time his sandwich arrived, and he ate it quickly. Just as he was swallowing the last of his lemonade, one of the children playing in the pool did a cannonball right next to where the boys were sitting. The cool water splashed them both, and they jumped up laughing.

"Boy, that feels good!" laughed Justin as he stood up and peeled off his shirt and jeans. "I'm going for a swim! Why don't you go get your trunks and come on in with me?" he asked Nate, while he signed his name and room number to the bill the waiter gave him.

Nate hesitated as he watched Justin poised on the edge of the pool. It flashed through his mind that his father might not approve. But just as quickly he realized that he enjoyed being with this friendly young American. Surely no harm could come from an innocent swim in the hotel pool.

"I'll be right back," he shouted, and took off running for the elevator.

Ten minutes later the boys were roughhousing in the pool, dunking each other, racing and diving, their shared pleasure finally ending any shyness between them.

Later, as they sat dangling their legs in the water that now felt warm to them, they talked easily. Nate said little about himself and Justin did not question him. But the two boys quickly discovered that they shared an interest in ancient history and, in particular, Egyptian history. They decided to meet early the next morning, and Nate would act as Justin's guide on a tour of the city and the Egyptian Museum. They also decided to try and speak Arabic as much as possible outside of the hotel.

After saying good night to Nate, Justin returned to his room and, exhausted, dropped into bed. When his parents looked in on him before they retired, he had a half-smile on his lips, and his hair, damp from swimming, was plastered to his head. Mrs. Sanders leaned over and brushed a kiss across her son's forehead. Their vacation was off to a good start.

CHAPTER 2

WHEN NATE LEFT THE POOL, HE TOOK THE ELEVATOR to the penthouse, high above the teeming city. Bursting into the suite, he headed directly for his room. Nate's father, seated at the desk, looked up from his writing with a frown creasing his brow.

"Where have you been?" he asked. "I expected you here an hour ago."

"I've been swimming. Can't you see that?"

Mr. Alistant, not used to the querulous tone in his son's voice, looked questioningly at him, then returned to his writing, pushing down the desire to question Nate further.

Nate felt a surge of relief, quickly followed by a pang of guilt. I should have told Father about Justin, he thought. He knew why he hadn't. He didn't want his relationship with Justin ended before it even got started. Nate understood the importance of secrecy. But his father should be able to trust him by now. On the other hand, he should be honest with his father.

Nate said good night, but at the door of his room he turned and said, "I met a boy at the pool tonight. He's an American and his name is Justin. Justin Sanders. He's nice." He added, "I'm going to take him to the museum tomorrow. Is that all right?"

Mr. Alistant started to protest and then changed his mind. "That's fine, Son, enjoy yourself. We only have a few more weeks here before we return."

"Thank you, Father."

Nate went into his room, and Mr. Alistant leaned back in his chair, a thoughtful look on his face. The closeness that he and Nate had shared while Nate was growing up seemed to have deteriorated recently. There were no angry words, no outward signs that things were different—and yet they were. It was good they'd be returning to their home soon.

His first instinct toward Nate's new friendship had been to terminate it as quickly and painlessly as possible. He knew that would be the wisest course. A year ago, Nate would have accepted his decision without question. Now? He wasn't sure.

Mr. Alistant stood up and started pacing up and down the luxurious suite. A friendship for just a few weeks wouldn't matter. Nate should have his friend. After all, I had my brother, he mused.

Moving in his usual decisive manner, Mr. Alistant picked up the phone and called the hotel dining room. He made reservations for three for dinner the next night, and then he retired to his own bedroom.

The next day, Nate woke early and hurried through his morning routine. He was trying hard to be quiet so as not to disturb his sleeping father. He hardly noticed the packing

19

boxes, the strange statues and artifacts, that made their luxury suite look like a storehouse. Their travels had led them to this ancient city over a year ago. Now their journey was almost at an end, and they would go home soon, taking with them all the treasures they had collected and, they hoped, the information they had long sought.

Nate found a piece of paper and wrote his father a note saying he would see him at dinner. Then he took some money from the wall safe and left the room, quietly closing the door behind him. He took the silent, swift elevator to the lobby and glanced into the dining room, looking around for Justin. Nate felt like taking his chances with the vendors on the street for their breakfast. He loved the spicy flavor of the local fare and the thick, sweet coffee you washed it down with. What a contrast to the safe but tasteless food in the dining room. Somehow he was sure that Justin would agree with him.

Nate leaned against the wall across from the elevator, waiting for his friend. He looked just like a young American in his light plaid shirt and jeans, the comfortable uniform that he loved as much as other young people all over the world. Nate's long, straight, black hair was tied back in a ponytail to keep it off his face in this hot climate. He hadn't had his hair cut in three years. When Nate and his father had arrived, their hair had been cut very close to their heads, but they decided to let it grow so they would be less conspicuous. Now Mr. Alistant visited a hair stylist once a week, and his surprisingly youthful head of black hair made him look younger than his actual age.

Nate watched the numbers above the elevator doors go swiftly from twelve to six, then to four, two. Finally, the doors slid apart and Justin stepped out.

"Hi. Have you been waiting long?" Justin asked shyly.

"No. I just got here. Are you hungry?" Nate turned and

started for the entrance. "I thought you might like to eat breakfast in the street."

"Great!" Justin agreed enthusiastically.

"Let me do the buying," Nate warned. "I'm used to bargaining and they won't overcharge me."

Justin was about to protest that he had done some bargaining in Saudi Arabia but decided to let Nate handle it.

When the boys stepped out onto the huge porch of the hotel, the sounds and heat of the city embraced them. The air was filled with a din of honking horns and the angry shouts of men driving donkey-pulled carts loaded with goods. Small children were curled up fast asleep amid the produce the farmers were hauling to market. The sidewalks swarmed with people, and on the corner there was a group of men placing bets.

All sorts of vendors crowded the street in front of the hotel: knife sharpeners, pot menders, basket sellers, vendors selling old clothes, old bottles, and even flowers. Nate bought bread, hot, from a vendor riding a bicycle, and coffee from a man who had a spirit stove, teakettle, spoons, and cups rattling on his back.

Justin's eyes were sparkling as he ate the delicious hot bread and sipped the sweet coffee. "I don't even like coffee, but this is different—really good," he said appreciatively.

Finished with breakfast, the boys quickly crossed the street to the Egyptian Museum, darting and dodging to avoid being hit. The wrought-iron gates of the museum were just being opened. At the entrance, there were the inevitable guides offering the boys their learned services. Justin was tempted to hire a guide on this, his first visit to the museum, but Nate hurried past the waiting men, saying to Justin, "I'm a better guide than anyone you'll find around here."

Justin paused in front of the building to look at a pool that was filled with lotus plants and papyrus, the two water plants that symbolized ancient Eqypt. Nate pointed at the papyrus and said, "That plant was literally extinct here up until a few years ago. Now, they're growing it again, but only in a few places. There's a Papyrus Institute in Cairo where it's grown and then made into paper. If we have time, I'll take you to see it. That's the place where Thor Heyerdahl had the material made for his boat, *Ra*. They've got pictures of him and the *Ra* at the Institute."

Nate and Justin walked up the few steps to the entrance, where they told the guards that they didn't have any cameras with them. Then they turned and went down a long hall filled with statues. Nate walked quickly ahead while Justin lingered to read the identification cards on the many statues. Finally, Nate came back, scowling, and said, "Listen! I'm your guide, and I know what's best to see. At the rate you're going, you won't see anything really important."

Justin reluctantly quickened his pace to match Nate's, and they finally reached the stairs at the end of the hall. They took the steps two at a time, and Justin was delighted to see a sign at the top of the stairs pointing to the rooms that held the Tutankhamon treasures.

Inside the first room of the Tutankhamon exhibit, Justin felt a stab of disappointment. The treasures that had thrilled millions were displayed in dusty, dirty glass and wood cases. Nate, sensing how Justin felt, said, "Part of the collection has just come back from a three-year tour of museums in the United States. I understand thousands and thousands of people stood in line for hours just to see it. The Egyptian Museum is going to use the money it made on the tour to re-do the entire museum. And it certainly needs it."

Justin stepped gingerly around a woman on her hands and knees who was washing the floor. He wanted to take a closer look at a collection of game boards displayed in a case. One in particular attracted his attention. It looked something like a narrow checkerboard on top of a box mounted on four short legs. As Justin bent over and squinted through the dusty glass, he marveled at what good condition it was in after more than 3,000 years.

"I bet it would be fun to play this game," he thought aloud, "if we had one and knew the rules."

Nate glanced at the display and then said, "But we can. I've got a game like that in my room. I'll teach you how."

Justin bent closer over the game board and said, "Look at that drawing there. It looks like a small bird."

Nate rubbed the dusty glass and stared intently at the spot Justin was pointing at. Then he said, "This game board was part of the exhibit that toured the United States. I've never had a chance to look at it closely before."

After studying the board for a few minutes, Nate pulled out a notebook and pencil and started drawing. When he had finished, he had faithfully reproduced the top of the checkered box, including the tiny bird. Justin sensed that he was extremely excited, but Nate did not explain and Justin didn't want to pry.

Just then, in the corner of the room, the scrub woman stood up wearily and carried her pail of very dirty water out the door. Nate glanced quickly around the now-empty room and then took a tiny camera out of his pocket.

Justin objected. "You were supposed to leave your camera downstairs."

"It's all right," Nate assured him. "Father and I have special permission to take pictures here."

Justin wasn't satisfied with Nate's glib answer because all the time he was taking pictures of the game board, he also kept glancing at the door to make sure nobody would come in and see what he was doing.

After Nate had finished with the pictures and was putting

his camera safely away, he explained. "It's just that, even with permission, it means a lot of forms to fill out. It would take too much of our time."

"But why do you want the pictures anyway?" Justin persisted.

"It's not important to anyone but Father and me," Nate said cryptically.

During the next few hours, Justin almost forgot the strange episode with the game board as Nate expertly led him to the most exciting things the museum had to offer. They saw the mummies, and the beautiful golden jewelry, and the famous model of the city of Tell el-Amarna, and the Amarna tablets. As they left the museum, Justin asked Nate why he only showed him the collection of the Eighteenth Dynasty.

"That's the period my father and I have been researching. So, of course, that's what I know the most about." Nate paused and then added shyly, "I guess I wanted to impress you. You weren't disappointed, were you? You can come back again and hire one of those guides for the rest of the museum."

"Gosh no, I'm not disappointed," Justin reassured Nate. "I haven't done much reading about the Eighteenth Dynasty, but of course I've heard of Akhenaton and his queen, Nefertiti. And the boy-king Tutankhamon. I'm really fascinated by the period, and I want to hear anything you can tell me about it."

Nate laughed. "I'll remind you of that later, when you start complaining about my lectures. Now let's go back to the hotel. I'm ready for lunch and a swim."

CHAPTER
3

 AFTER CHANGING INTO THEIR TRUNKS, JUSTIN AND NATE met at the pool and ordered a lunch of thick sand-wiches and cold lemonade. While they were eating, Justin spotted his dad walking toward the tennis court, racquet under his arm. Mr. Sanders saw the boys and changed direction, heading for their table.

Justin made the introductions carefully. "Dad, I want you to meet my friend Nate. Nate, this is my father, Jud Sanders."

Nate stood up and politely shook hands with Justin's father. "How do you do, Mr. Sanders."

"Hello there, Nate." Mr. Sanders pulled out a chair to sit down. "Mind if I join you?"

"Please do, sir," Nate said as he sat down again.

"Justin tells me you're acting as his guide. You must have lived here for quite a while to be able to do that," Mr. Sanders said admiringly.

"We've been here for a little over a year now," Nate replied.

"Hmm... Over a year." Mr. Sanders raised his eyebrows as he added, "All that time here at the Hilton?"

Justin felt his face redden. He knew what his father was getting at. The next thing he'd be asking what Nate's father did for a living.

"Yes, sir," Nate explained, "We probably should have taken an apartment, but Father felt it would be simpler for two bachelors like us to live here at the hotel."

"I see," Mr. Sanders said. "And what does your father do?"

Justin groaned.

Nate glanced at Justin as he said, "He's sort of an ambassador—and a historian."

Justin's curiosity overcame his embarrassment. "A real ambassador?" he asked excitedly. "From what country?"

Now Nate's face darkened as he tried to explain.

"Not exactly an ambassador. Maybe what you'd call a good-will ambassador, and we're from...." Nate hesitated. "We're from Bimini, a small island in the Caribbean," he finished in a rush.

Justin was sure Nate wasn't telling the truth—at least, not the whole truth. Although he was curious, he also wanted to save Nate from any more of his dad's prying questions. So he interrupted, saying, "Is that man over there looking for you, Dad?"

"Where?" Mr. Sanders looked across the courtyard to where Justin was pointing. "No. That's not my partner. But I should get out to the court. Say, could I interest you two in a game of tennis this afternoon?" he asked. "We could play doubles."

Relieved at the sudden shift in conversation, Justin said, "I'm sorry, Dad, but we've already made plans for the rest of the day."

"I'd like to play some time," Nate spoke up, "but I'm not

very good. Maybe you could help me with my backhand."

"Any time, son, any time." Mr. Sanders gave Nate a fatherly pat on the shoulder as he got up to leave.

"What good condition your dad is in!" Nate exclaimed, as he watched Mr. Sanders thread his way through the tables to the tennis courts.

"He ought to be. He spends enough time working at it," Justin said spitefully.

Nate raised his eyebrows as he realized he had just touched a sore spot as far as Justin was concerned. Tactfully, he suggested that they take their swim.

The temperature was soaring and the cool water of the pool felt soothing to their sunburned skins. After swimming lazily for 15 minutes, the two boys got out and sat on the side of the pool with their legs in the water. Justin asked Nate to tell him more about King Tut and the Eighteenth Dynasty. "Was Tutankhamon Nefertiti's son?" he asked.

"No," Nate answered. "She helped raise him, but historians pretty much agree that he was Akhenaton's half-brother and, later, his son-in-law. Tut was married to Akhenaton and Nefertiti's daughter when he was pharaoh."

"Tut wasn't pharaoh for very long, was he?"

"Only about nine years—he died when he was just nineteen. Tutankhamon wasn't a very important pharaoh, but Akhenaton was. He and Nefertiti ruled one of the largest kingdoms in the ancient world. Their ancestor, Thutmose III, had built up a great empire through military conquest. Akhenaton's father, Amenhotep III, was Thutmose's great-grandson, and he expanded Egypt's trade and built many temples and monuments. Akhenaton inherited his father's kingdom around 1370 B.C. Of course, then his name was Amenhotep IV. He changed it to Akhenaton when he changed his religion, which is a fascinating story in itself."

Justin laughed. "Hold on a minute. I'm getting mixed up with all these names. Tutankhamon, Thutmose, *two* Imhoteps..."

"Not Imhotep—Amenhotep! Imhotep is another very famous Egyptian, but he's from a much earlier time—about a thousand years before Akhenaton and Tutankhamon. I'll tell you about him when we go to see the pyramids at Giza."

Justin's eyes shone as he thought about what they would see tomorrow. But they still had a full afternoon ahead of them today. They spent it fighting the crowds on Cairo's transportation system and visiting the Papyrus Institute. On their way back to the hotel, Nate insisted that Justin must see the Alabaster Mosque, a beautiful building built entirely from alabaster. The mosque was 500 years old and seemed very young compared to the rest of Egypt's monuments. Justin thought about his own country's recent 200th birthday and marveled once again at the long and colorful history of Egypt.

Back at the hotel, the boys separated, planning to meet again after dinner. When Nate returned to the penthouse suite, his father was there working in the study. Nate burst into the room and dropped the drawing of the game board on the desk in front of him.

"What's this?" Mr. Alistant asked, annoyed at being interrupted.

"Look at it closely, Father. See, down in the lower part. What do you make of it?" Nate said as he pointed at the small bird he had drawn.

"Why, it's an ibis. But what's so important about it? We must have seen thousands of them." Mr. Alistant handed the paper back to Nate as if to dismiss it.

Nate couldn't keep the excitement out of his voice as he said, "Justin, my new friend, found it. It's on one of Tutankhamon's game boards in the museum. I've seen versions of that same game many times, but I never noticed an ibis before. I took pictures of it that I'm going to develop. You may not think it's important, but I do!"

Mr. Alistant wearily put down his pen and said, "Don't get your hopes up, Nathan. This will probably be a deadend just like so many of the other leads we tracked down."

Nate refused to be discouraged. "Do you mind if I follow this one up by myself?" he asked.

"If you want to. But you must be very careful about your new friend," his father cautioned. "Don't ever reveal to him the object of our search."

"Oh, Father! How stupid do you think I am!"

Mr. Alistant then softened his criticism by saying, "I've made reservations for three in the dining room for dinner tonight. I want to meet this extraordinary new friend of yours. Call Justin and ask him to join us."

"That's wonderful! You'll like him—and it is better to have another pair of eyes helping me. After all, he found this!"

After calling Justin, Nate went into his room to study the drawing again. He took out an exact duplicate of the game in the museum and laid the paper over it. It meant nothing.

Maybe Father is right, and this is another meaningless lead, he thought. But no! Intuitively, he was sure about the importance of the ibis.

That evening in the dining room, Justin studied the menu without interest. Funny, he'd been so hungry just an hour ago. Now, he was so nervous he'd lost his appetite.

Mr. Alistant looked at Justin—in fact, seemed to study him closely. He saw a sixteen-year-old boy, nearly six feet tall, with sandy-colored hair and light, clear blue eyes. He also noticed Justin's flushed face and correctly guessed that his young guest was terribly uncomfortable.

Mr. Alistant smiled as he said, "I've looked forward to meeting you, Justin. Nate tells me you two have a lot in common."

"Oh yes, sir!" Justin replied. "I'm interested in ancient history, but I'm nowhere near as good at it as Nate. It's fun, though, to have a friend who gets turned on to the same things I do."

"Turned on?"

"That's just a figure of speech, sir. It means you really dig something," Justin explained.

"Dig..."

Justin laughed. "You couldn't have spent too much time in America, or you'd know that one. 'Dig' means to like something a lot."

"Oh yes. I see." Nate's father quickly turned his attention to the menu. "May I recommend the lamb? It's excellent."

Nate grinned at Justin. He had enjoyed immensely the exchange between his father and his new friend.

Later that night Nate's thoughts returned to the game board and the meaning of the ibis. Back in his room, he studied the photographs he'd developed earlier and compared them to the drawing. Then he took out a fresh sheet of paper and carefully re-drew the ibis, correcting its position by a fraction of an inch. He laid the corrected version on top of his own game board, which was identical in every way to the one in the museum... except for the ibis.

"It has to mean something. It just *has* to."

CHAPTER
4

EARLY THE NEXT MORNING, NATE AND JUSTIN WERE standing on a busy Cairo street corner.

"These buses never stop," Nate said, "so we have to be alert when we see one coming."

It took a regular decathlon of running, jumping, and vaulting to board the bus, and afterwards, the boys were breathless from the exercise and from laughing. The bus had no seats, but Nate and Justin enjoyed the challenge of keeping their balance during the jolting ride.

There was no opportunity for conversation in the crowded, noisy bus, so Justin stared, enthralled, out the window. The street was clogged. Cars and trucks and donkeys pulling carts plowed through the crowds. Men and women passed by carrying incredible loads on their heads. Justin saw one man with about fifty shoe boxes lashed together, balanced precariously on his head. The bus also passed a funeral procession that became swallowed in the crowd so that only the coffin, carried high, could be seen.

The bus load had thinned out enough by the time they reached the Street of the Pyramids, so the boys had a better view of everything. Nothing had prepared Justin for the thrill of seeing the Great Pyramid suddenly looming up before them as they turned the corner. It was absolutely, geometrically, perfect—and it looked so close. Maybe a block away at the most.

As the bus continued on its route, Justin realized that the pyramid was still some distance away. He also saw that, behind the first pyramid, there were two others. One had a sort of cap on it and was almost, but not quite, as big as the first. The third one was noticeably smaller.

Finally, the bus pulled to a stop. When the boys got off, they were surrounded by peddlers hawking their wares of jewelry, tiny leather camels, alabaster scarabs, and hundreds of other tourist items. Nate was very adept at saying "la," which means "no" in Arabic, firmly enough to be let alone. Leaving the peddlers behind, he approached the stables where the camels were kept, avoiding the donkeys and horse-driven carriages available to take the tourists up to the pyramids. He quickly negotiated for two camels and the drivers to lead them.

Justin's camel was resting on its knees as the driver helped him into the saddle and then saw that his feet were firmly fixed in the stirrups. The driver, who was named Hassim, poked the camel with his walking staff, and the camel promptly rose to its feet. Justin laughed as he towered over Nate, who hadn't yet gotten on his camel.

"What's his name?" Justin asked in Arabic, surprising the driver.

"Moses," answered Hassim, who then started asking Justin questions about where he was from, how he knew the language, about his family. Justin liked the camel driver and resolved to tip him generously.

As soon as Nate had mounted his camel, they set off on the short ride to the pyramids. Justin decided that riding a camel was a little like riding a horse, except that you were up a lot higher and the gait was more rolling and slow.

Instead of stopping at the Great Pyramid, Nate motioned the drivers on to the second, smaller, pyramid. They arrived just in time to join a group of fifteen tourists about to be led into the dark entrance by a guide.

"Too bad!" said Nate. "I wanted to go in by ourselves."

"That's all right," Justin replied. "I don't mind a bit." Secretly, he was rather relieved to be among this group of familiar-looking Americans.

"Lower your heads as you enter, please," shouted the guide.

When Justin stepped into the surprising coolness of the entrance, he found himself in a passageway only about four feet high, which led down into the pyramid. By the time they reached the end of the first passageway, Justin could hardly wait to stand upright and ease his aching back. Unfortunately, no one had told him that pyramids had been built for small people, so he cracked his head painfully on the 5'6" ceiling of the adjoining corridor. The group continued along this level corridor until they reached a huge room. There they all gathered around the guide, who explained to them that the room was at the exact center of the base of the pyramid and that it had been the burial place of Chephron, son of Cheops, who was the builder of the Great Pyramid.

After admiring the burial chamber, empty for centuries due to the work of grave robbers, the tourists went back out the same way they had entered. Both boys were temporarily blinded as they emerged into the sunlight. Justin turned to Nate and asked, "Why did we go into this pyramid and not the great one of Cheops?"

Nate looked mysterious and replied, "Because I'm taking you into that one myself. There are too many tourists around today, so I settled for Chephron's pyramid first. I also want to tell you about the real history of the Great Pyramid before you go into it."

"You mean we're not even going into it today?" Justin sounded disappointed.

"Trust me, Justin. You really shouldn't go into the Great Pyramid with a whole group of tourists. We'll get up before dawn tomorrow and come back here. After I take you into the pyramid, we'll even climb it! Let's go now to see the Sphinx and have lunch. Later, we'll take a cab to Sakhara so you can see the famous Step Pyramid. That's the one most historians agree was the first to be built. I'll tell you about the brilliant man who built it while we're eating."

The Great Sphinx, sprawling on the sand near the pyramid of Chephron, awed Justin almost as much as the pyramid itself. Half human, half lion, its great face battered by the passage of time, the Sphinx looked as mysterious as the legends claimed. After standing in the blazing sun and gazing up at its towering shape, Justin and Nate were more than ready to take a break from ancient history and have lunch.

They went to the Mene House, which was just a short distance from the pyramids. It had been built in the nineteenth century as a hunting lodge for the king of Egypt. Near the end of the century, the lodge had been made into a hotel, and the guests amused themselves by sitting on the porch and watching tourists climb aboard the camels to make the trip to the pyramids.

In the elegant and cool dining room of the Mene House, the boys waited for their lunch to be served. The first course was a delicious clear lamb soup accompanied by hot crusty rolls. Next came a salad of tomatoes and cucumbers. After eating most of his salad, Nate pushed the plate away and leaned across the table toward Justin.

"Imhotep," he said. "Remember, I was going to tell you about him."

"He's the one who built the Step Pyramid?"

"That's right. During the reign of King Zoser, around 2700 B.C. That was the Third Dynasty, at the beginning of the period known as the Old Kingdom. Imhotep was an adviser to the king and a wise and brilliant man. He was a writer, an astronomer, a physician, and, of course, an architect. Imhotep left his mark on the Egyptian culture, which made fantastic and rapid achievements during the Old Kingdom."

Justin frowned. "Are you suggesting that Imhotep had something to do with the development of Egyptian culture? That he was the man behind the scenes during that period?"

"Exactly!" Nate replied. "Except he hasn't really been given credit for it. Oh, he was made a god by the Egyptians later, but historians today haven't paid that much attention to him. I'm fascinated by Imhotep and others like him in Egyptian history—the 'people behind the scenes,' as you put it. The ones who caused things to happen."

"How about the Eighteenth Dynasty? Was there someone behind the scenes during Akhenaton's reign?"

Nate hesitated before answering. It was almost as if he were divulging some deep secret when he slowly said, "Yes, there was. Aye, the Grand Vizier."

"Tell me about him," urged Justin.

"Some other time," Nate answered. "Today, we're concentrating on Imhotep and the Old Kingdom. Let's finish lunch. We can catch a cab here at the hotel to take us to Sakhara."

Justin eagerly attacked the dessert that had been placed in front of him. It was like a flat cake, but when he bit into it, he discovered it was soaked in a sweet, honey-like liqueur.

Fortified by lunch, the two boys were ready to continue their exploration. In the taxi approaching Sakhara, Nate seemed transfixed by the sight of the beautiful Step Pyramid, coming closer and closer on the horizon. Justin had gotten involved in a conversation with Said, their driver.

"You're twenty-five years old and you already have three children?" Justin asked incredulously. "Did you go to school?"

"I only went for two years. My father needed me to work in the fields," Said replied.

"But when did you learn to speak English so well?" Justin asked.

Said shrugged and said, "You learn what you must. Driving a taxi, I must be able to speak English." He added proudly, "Also Italian, German, and French!"

Justin was impressed. Imagine being fluent in four languages plus your own, with only two years of education.

When the small taxi pulled to a stop near the entrance of the pyramid complex, there was no one else in sight. Nate jumped out, saying, "We're in luck! No tourists. Hurry up!"

He asked the driver to wait for them and then took off at a swift pace. Justin scrambled after him, feeling the ever-present sand sifting into his sandals. They walked along a magnificent wall over 30 feet high and more than a mile long, which enclosed the complex. Dwarfing the wall was the pyramid itself. Nate told Justin that it was 413 feet by 344 feet at the base and that it soared upwards in six giant terraces for almost 200 feet.

The boys entered the pyramid by walking down a colonnade and then through huge stone doors left perpetually ajar. Inside, they followed a long sloping corridor until they found themselves looking down into a pit 90 feet deep. At the bottom lay the burial room. The hole in the top to admit the pharaoh's body had once been sealed by a granite plug weighing several tons. From this room many corridors branched out. They led down and down, a hundred feet under the sandy desert to where rooms had been carved out of solid rock.

It was so hushed that Justin jumped when Nate started talking.

"Most historians believe that this is the first and oldest pyramid. My father and I don't believe that is true, and there are a few historians who agree with us."

"What do you mean?" Justin asked.

"When we go to see the Great Pyramid at Giza, I'll explain what I mean." Nate was being deliberately mysterious. "Just remember, this pyramid was built by one of the greatest men who ever lived—Imhotep."

"Where is Imhotep's tomb?" asked Justin.

"It's never been found." Nate's reply was final and signaled an end to their conversation.

As they left the pyramid to return to the car, they came upon a group of tourists gathered around a guide who obviously loved the sound of his own voice. Carefully avoiding the group, the boys passed near an old man dressed in a flowing black robe and holding a staff in his hand. Justin's eyes met and held the old man's, who gestured at the noisy guide and said in Arabic, "An empty vessel makes much noise." Justin grinned and nodded agreement.

On the long, hot ride back to Cairo in Said's taxi, the boys, tired by now, were silent. Justin's thoughts turned again to what Nate had told his dad the day before. Ambassador from Bimini?

Suddenly, he turned to Nate and said, "You're not really from Bimini are you? I just don't buy that. Where are you from anyway?"

Nate sighed and said, "That was so stupid of me. Oh, we've been to Bimini. In fact, we were there for a few weeks before we came here. I guess that's why the name came to me."

"Listen, Nate," Justin interrupted. "You don't have to tell me where you're from if you don't want to."

"I'd like to tell you, Justin, but I've promised my father." Nate spread his hands helplessly. "He wouldn't let me see you anymore if he thought I'd told you even this much."

Justin, alarmed at the idea of losing Nate's friendship, quickly reassured him that he would ask no more questions. Of course, Justin couldn't promise that he would stop wondering and speculating about his friend's mysterious past.

Said let the boys off in front of their hotel, and as Justin was getting out, Nate made arrangements for the driver to pick them up at the same place at four o'clock sharp the next morning.

After a swim and a snack, the boys turned in early, their clocks set for 3:30 A.M. But Justin couldn't relax. Although he was tired, sleep was slow in coming. He kept thinking about the strange conversation he'd had with Nate in the taxi. Where *did* he come from? And what did his father do? Was he really a "good-will ambassador"? Or could he be ... a spy? A political refugee? Someone running from the law?

Finally, worn out by his confused thoughts, Justin fell asleep.

CHAPTER 5

JUSTIN WAS LYING ON A COUCH BESIDE A BEAUTIFUL Egyptian princess. She picked up a bell from the elaborately carved table next to her and started ringing it for a servant. She kept on ringing and ringing. Justin put out a hand to stop her when, suddenly, she disappeared. He sat up, fully awake, to find his alarm clock ringing and ringing. When he pushed in the button on the clock, the noise finally stopped.

Dressing quickly, Justin ran down the stairs and arrived in the lobby at the same time that Nate stepped out of the elevator—exactly 4 A.M. Nate pulled a couple of hard rolls from his pocket and said, "These will have to do for now. We'll have a big breakfast at the Jolle Ville when we're through visiting the Great Pyramid."

"What's the Jolle Ville? A restaurant?" asked Justin.

"It's a Swiss-owned hotel out near the pyramids at Giza.

They serve a breakfast buffet there that's the best in Egypt," replied Nate.

Justin gulped down the roll and felt hungrier than before.

When Nate and Justin walked out into the cool pre-dawn darkness, they found Said patiently waiting for them next to his cab. During the ride through the surprisingly busy streets, Justin asked Nate to explain what he had meant about the Step Pyramid at Sakhara not being the oldest pyramid.

Nate settled back into the seat and said, "Some people think that the Great Pyramid at Giza is the oldest."

"Didn't I read in my guidebook that the age of the Great Pyramid had been confirmed by finding Cheops' name carved on it somewhere?"

"Yes, his name was found, in a place where it had to be put while the pyramid was being built. And we are fairly sure that a pharaoh named Cheops—Khufu in Egyptian—reigned during the Fourth Dynasty, about 2580 B.C. That's why most historians date the pyramid from that period. But my father and I don't believe it. We think that it was built much earlier."

"What reasons do you have?" demanded Justin.

"Well, for one thing, there's no reference to the Great Pyramid *anywhere* in Egyptian literature. This lack of information seems incredible, considering what an enormous building project it must have been. Of course, all the information could have been destroyed when the great library at Alexandria was burned in Julius Caesar's time, but you'd think there would be some record among the inscriptions that have survived on the temples and monuments."

"But how does the lack of information show that the Great Pyramid wasn't built during the Fourth Dynasty?"

"By the time of the Fourth Dynasty, Egyptian writing was highly developed. Records were kept of all kinds of important matters. If the pyramid had been built then, some record would have been made of how it was built. The reason there was no record was that the people of the Fourth Dynasty didn't *know* how it was built! The pyramid had been constructed before Cheops ruled Egypt."

"I guess that makes sense. But how do you explain Cheops' name being on the pyramid?"

"Repeated use of a pharaoh's name is very common in Egyptian history," Nate explained patiently. "Remember all the Amenhoteps and Thutmoses I told you about earlier?"

"Sure! So you believe that there was a ruler named Cheops earlier than the Fourth Dynasty and that the pyramid was built during his reign. But *when?*"

"My father and I believe that the pyramid was built before the great flood—"

Justin interrupted. "The flood! You mean the one described in the Bible?"

"And in the literature of a lot of other civilizations as well. Do you know that early explorers were said to have found seashells at all levels of the Great Pyramid and even a half inch of salt covering the inner chambers?"

"Okay, the Great Pyramid was built before the flood, whenever that was. But who built it?"

"We believe that it was the product of a great civilization that existed for thousands of years early in human history. This super race used its advanced technology to build the Great Pyramid and to make it a repository of scientific information."

"Wow! But I don't understand..."

"We're here!" Nate exclaimed as the taxi pulled up in front of the entrance to the pyramid. There were no camels around at this early hour, but there were the inevitable guides.

"When do they sleep?" Justin wondered aloud.

"Let's walk around the pyramid first," Nate said, "and I'll give you some statistics that will astonish you. The Great

Pyramid covers thirteen and a half acres of ground." Nate paused to let that sink in and then continued. "It rises to the height of a forty-story building. From the top, you can't throw a stone or even shoot an arrow past its base. You'll find that out when we climb it. There are two and a half million stones in the pyramid, weighing from two to seventy tons apiece. Originally it had a cap of gold that reflected the sun and the moon for many miles around."

Justin reached out and touched the surface of the pyramid. It was very rough, yet from a distance, it looked smooth. Nate explained that this rough surface had originally been covered with smooth, tight-fitting slabs of limestone, which had been removed over the centuries and used to construct many of the buildings in Cairo.

The two boys turned the corner of the giant edifice while Nate recited more statistics. "The entire structure is oriented with such accuracy to the exact directions of the compass that once a year each of the four sides is lit by the sun. And here's something even more amazing. Map-makers have found that this pyramid stands exactly in the center of the world—not the known world of Cheops' time, but the entire world as we know it today!"

"Incredible!" Justin said.

Nate, enjoying his rapt audience, elaborated. "The only way the pyramid's builders could have picked this spot would have been to survey earth from space, make a global map, project it flat, and then draw lines through the precise middle of the map's land surface!"

Nate paused again for effect—and also for a breath. They continued their walk, and in fifteen minutes they were back at the entrance.

"Let's go in now," Nate said, "and I'll tell you more when we come out."

The boys walked 62 feet down a descending corridor, then entered another corridor with a very low ceiling. They had to go on all fours along this passageway, which ascended to the very heart of the pyramid. There they entered the Grand Gallery, 153 feet long, with walls that sloped inward to support a ceiling 28 feet high. They moved on into an antechamber and finally into the pharaoh's funerary chamber itself, carved out of dark granite and containing the empty sarcophagus.

Here the two boys paused to rest a minute. Then Nate said, "My father and I believe that the Grand Gallery may have served as a kind of telescope. Through it, a series of observers could accurately note the transit of heavenly bodies. By looking down the descending passage into a reflecting pool, an ancient astronomer could have seen the exact moment of a star's transit. Your own Naval Observatory uses the same system today—only they use a pool of mercury instead of water."

Justin was impressed by Nate's explanation of the pyramid's significance. "I'm no expert," he said, "but it looks to me as if the Great Pyramid could have been built by a very early, very advanced civilization. Why don't historians believe it?"

"Because," Nate replied sadly, "they can't imagine the existence of any culture that would have been superior to their own."

With that, he turned to leave. Justin followed him closely along the dim corridors. When they emerged, they found it was full daylight outside.

"Now we climb it," Nate said excitedly. "Let's go!"

The boys began to climb the majestic but dilapidated northern slope, stepping on the edges of the blocks that made up the outer surface of the pyramid. The steps were narrow and, to make matters worse, they were very high—about three feet. Each step was just a few inches higher than the average human leg and knee could negotiate easily.

When Justin and Nate finally got to the top, they were standing on a level platform created by the absence of the capstone that had originally formed the peak of the Great Pyramid. Hot, tired, and triumphant, they looked down at the desert floor, 451 feet below, and at the pyramid of Chephron, which they had entered yesterday.

"Here." Nate handed Justin a stone. "Try and see if you can clear the base."

Justin mocked a baseball pitcher's windup and threw as hard as he could. He saw the stone hit against the side of the pyramid about two-thirds of the way down.

"It looks so easy," he said wonderingly. "I'm sure glad you told me no one else could do it either."

It was easier going down, but still tricky. When they were once again at the base of the pyramid, they noticed some construction going on.

"Do you know what they're building?" Justin asked. "It looks like a large boat."

"That's what it is—a solar boat," Nate replied.

"A solar boat?"

"You've seen them before," Nate said. "On the wall paintings in the tombs. Even the King Tut treasures included several small solar boats. The dead pharaohs were supposed to use solar boats to travel across the sky. In King Tut's time, only small model boats were provided, but during the Old Kingdom, they buried full-size boats in front of the pyramid for the pharaoh to use. Archaeologists discovered several of these boats only about twenty years ago, and it created quite a stir. This boat-shaped building will be used to house the remains of the solar boats."

"Solar boats," Justin mused. "And we thought we were so advanced with our space program."

Nate laughed and said, "Remember, these were only used

by dead pharaohs. It was just part of their religion." He paused and then said reflectively, "The boats could have been based on real space ships, though. I wonder."

As promised, Said was waiting for them in his taxi. During the short ride to the Jolle Ville, the boys invited him to join them for breakfast.

The Jolle Ville looks just like a modern American motel, Justin thought as they walked up to its entrance. It wasn't nearly as grand as the Hilton or the Mene House, but he could see the well-known Swiss efficiency at work.

In the large and attractive dining room, there were long tables set up with a variety of fruits, juices, meats, and scrambled eggs. Along with the usual hard rolls, there were raisin-filled honey rolls and toast. The boys and Said helped themselves to generous portions of everything and sat down to enjoy it. After breakfast, they strolled through the hotel's beautiful gardens and looked at the inviting swimming pools.

"When we get back to our hotel, would you show me how to play King Tut's game?" Justin asked Nate.

"All right. We'd better get started back," Nate said as he turned to leave.

The ride to the hotel was quiet. Justin was deep in thought over all he'd seen and heard this morning, and Nate, too, seemed to be lost in his own mysterious thoughts.

"Let me pay for the cab today," Justin insisted when they arrived. Nate didn't argue as Justin pulled out his wallet and spent some of his carefully saved money.

It seemed to Justin, a trifle enviously, that Nate had an unlimited supply of money to spend. His father must be awfully rich, he thought, as he watched Nate push the elevator button for the penthouse floor.

Mr. Alistant was gone when the boys walked through the luxurious suite to Nate's only slightly less elegant room. Justin saw the game board on a table and recognized it immediately. It looked like an exact duplicate of the game in the museum. Where in the world did he get it? Justin wondered. He also saw the drawing that Nate had made of the game board at the museum lying carelessly across the top of the duplicate board.

"Why did you get so excited about this?" Justin asked, pointing to the drawing.

"There's something special about it," Nate replied. "Several game boards were found in Tut's tomb, but all the others I've seen have only five decorated tiles on the playing surface. Mine is like that, and I assumed that the one sent on the tour—the one you noticed in the museum—would be the same. But it has *six* decorated tiles, and the sixth tile has the ibis on it."

"So? What's so special about an ibis?"

"I'm not sure, but I have a feeling about it," Nate said slowly as he studied the drawing for the hundredth time.

"What about those photographs you took?" Justin asked. "They might show something that you missed in the drawing. You could even try enlarging them..."

"I never thought of that!" Nate's excitement was obvious even though he attempted to cover it up. "It might be interesting—but right now I want to show you how to play the game."

Justin couldn't get over the feeling of being rushed through the learning of the game, which was quite difficult. In less than an hour, he was out of the beautiful suite and back in his own room. He really didn't mind, though, because all of a sudden, he was extremely tired. As he dozed off, he wondered if the beautiful Egyptian princess would reappear in his dreams.

CHAPTER
6

NATE REALIZED HE WAS BEING RUDE TO JUSTIN WHEN he deliberately rushed him through the game and out the door. But he couldn't help himself. There was something he had to do, and Justin had given him the idea. Twice, this new friend had opened important doors for him—first, when he noticed the ibis on King Tut's game board, and now, when he suggested enlarging the photographs.

As soon as Justin left, Nate hurried to the darkroom, which had been installed the very first month that the Alistants had lived in the hotel. It was beautifully equipped, including the best enlarger money could buy. Nate had worked with this marvelous instrument before, enlarging details from photographs that his father had taken in temples, tombs, and museums. Now he had something of his own to enlarge.

Selecting the clearest negative of the pictures he had taken,

Nate placed it carefully in the holder of the enlarger. Then he focused the image of the game board, adjusting the lens until only the ibis could be seen. After he was satisfied with the focus, Nate put a piece of print paper in the enlarger easel. Now to choose the proper exposure time. Since this was an enlargement of a short-range picture, he wanted to over-expose the negative. There! The exposure had been made. Nate removed the paper from the easel and slid it deftly into the tray of developer.

The next two to three minutes were endless. As Nate gently rocked the tray of developer, he saw the print paper beginning to change. In the eerie light of the darkroom, the pale grey image of the ibis slowly emerged from its watery bath. Nate held his breath. The image darkened, became more precise, and...

"It looks like a map!"

Nate could hardly wait to finish the developing process. It seemed to take forever to fix the print, then wash and dry it, but at last it was finished. Nate hurried to his father's desk and put the enlargement under a high intensity lamp. It *was* a map! Drawn within the body of the ibis was a tiny but distinct map.

Nate looked intently at the drawing. It looked like a map of Egypt. There, up at the top—that had to be the Delta. And that long, squiggly line must be the Nile River. He traced the line with his finger, and about two-thirds of the way down, he noticed some kind of mark on what would be the west bank of the Nile. When Nate looked at the mark with a magnifying glass, he saw that it was actually a tiny drawing of a bird.

"The ibis again!" he whispered to himself.

Excitedly, Nate pulled a long cylinder out of the back of the desk. He opened it and carefully spread it out, putting paper weights at all four corners. It was a large map of the earth showing only land areas—no political boundaries were marked. Nate's eyes moved quickly to the area around the Nile River. It was definitely the same as the map on the game board. When Nate got a modern map of the area, he found that the figure of the ibis marked a spot just above the Second Cataract of the Nile, not far from the site of the Temple of Abu Simbel.

Nate was deep in thought when his father walked into the room.

"What have we here?" Mr. Alistant asked. "I thought you and your friend would be all day at the pyramids."

"Father! Come and see what I have discovered!" Nate pointed to the enlarged print of the ibis lying innocently on top of the large map of the world. But Mr. Alistant saw only the map and became very angry. "You know you're not to touch this, ever!" he said accusingly. "Don't tell me you've shown this to Justin. That's inexcusable!" He was very shaken.

Nate had never seen his father so angry. He hurriedly reassured him that Justin had not seen the map and then tried to draw his attention to the photograph. But Mr. Alistant had already turned away. Wearily, he dropped down into a chair and ran his fingers through his thick hair.

Nate felt sorry for his father. All of a sudden, he looked as old as he was. Nate didn't want to see him disappointed again. Why tell him about the ibis map at all—at least not before the clue was checked out. If it turned out to be a false lead, then his father would never have to know about it.

Mr. Alistant had by now recovered his composure. He asked Nate, "What did you want to show me?"

"It's nothing very important—just something on the game board that seems to point to an area along the river south of Abu Simbel. If you don't mind, I would like to go down there with Justin and see what we can find."

Mr. Alistant looked alarmed again at the mention of Justin's name. Nate hurried to add, "Justin doesn't know anything. And he won't know anything either. If something comes from this, I'll phone you straight away. If nothing comes from it, Justin and I will have a good time anyway."

Nate's enthusiasm was persuasive, even though Mr. Alistant was sure that this Abu Simbel thing would prove to be just another frustrating lead. He himself didn't have the courage to face another disappointment, but Nate was eager to try. He found himself warming to the idea. "It's all right with me, if Justin's parents will allow him to go." He added, "You realize, don't you, that your chances of finding anything are very small?"

Nate replied on his way out of the room. "Yes, sir, I do. But I still want to try."

In his own room, Nate quickly dialed Justin's number. The phone rang several times before Justin roused out of the deep, dreamless sleep he'd fallen into.

"Hello?" he answered in a voice dulled by sleep.

"Justin! It's me. Nate. First of all, do you think your parents would let you go on a trip with me? Down to Aswan and Luxor and Abu Simbel?"

"Well, uh, gee, I don't know," stammered Justin.

"Ask them. Right now," Nate insisted.

"They're not here now. I'll ask them when they get back." Justin was beginning to wake up.

"Also," Nate continued, "do you know anything at all about scuba diving? It's important."

"Well, yeah. In fact, I'm pretty good at it," Justin answered immodestly.

"Good! Tomorrow we'll get the equipment, and you'll give me some lessons. By Tuesday we should be ready to leave for

Luxor." Nate hastened to add, "If it's all right with your parents."

Nate hung up abruptly, and Justin lay with his hands behind his head, waiting for his body to come as fully awake as his mind was. How exciting, he thought. He'd get to see the Valley of the Kings, the Aswan Dam, beautiful Lake Nasser, and the Temple at Abu Simbel. His thoughts were racing ahead. All of a sudden he frowned. Scuba diving! In Lake Nasser? It was another of Nate's mysteries, but by now Justin had learned to relax and enjoy them.

Justin's thoughts were interrupted by the sound of his door opening. He looked up and saw his mother smiling at him in the doorway.

"Good. You're awake," she said, as she came and sat on the edge of his bed. "I'm so happy you're having a good time. You are, aren't you?" she asked.

"The best ever, Mom," he replied. "How about you?"

"Me too," she agreed.

She looked so pretty and so young sitting there in the soft late afternoon light filtering through the blinds.

"Tonight, your father and I want you to eat dinner with us." Expecting him to object, she hurried on. "We're joining some friends for dinner at eight, and they have a daughter almost your age who will be there too. So, please, do me a favor, and be nice to her."

Justin looked away. He hated these contrived boy-girl relationships they kept putting him into. But then, he thought, maybe if I do this for them, they'll let me go with Nate.

He turned to his mother, gave her a big smile, and said, "Sure. It might be fun. I'll be ready whenever you are."

Justin spent a lot of time getting ready for dinner that night. He took a long shower and even shaved the annoying stubble on his chin. While he was combing his hair, Mr. Sanders rapped on the bathroom door and said, "Hurry up! We're already five minutes late, and the Bronsons will be waiting."

Justin ran the comb through his hair one last time, smiled, and then frowned at his reflection. Finally he switched off the light and stepped out

"Don't you look nice!" his mother said with an approving look at his light blue denim suit. Mrs. Sanders was dressed in a gallabeo, one of the robes worn by both men and women in Egypt, which she had purchased just that afternoon. It was pale blue, the same shade as her eyes, and trimmed in white braid. Mr. Sanders looked as if he were dressed for a business meeting in his dark suit and polka dot tie.

Together, the three of them took the elevator to the roof of the Hilton, where they entered the elegant Belvedere Supper Club. The maître d' led them expertly across the crowded room to the large table near the window where the Sanders' friends were waiting.

"Mr. and Mrs. Bronson, Emily and Don, this is my son, Justin." Mr. Sanders seemed proud of his son as he introduced him to the Bronsons. Justin shook hands with the typical American couple and then glanced at their daughter. She wasn't typical at all!

"This is our daughter, Merit." Mr. Bronson's voice had a note of pride in it too.

Justin's bashfulness suddenly returned as he said, "Hi. I'm glad to meet you."

"Justin. That's an unusual name," Merit said, holding out her hand. Her hand was small, yet its grip was firm.

"Your name is unusual too," Justin observed. "Is it a family name?" He was glad they were seated next to each other, and he hoped his face wasn't as red as it felt.

"No. It's Egyptian," Merit replied. "Mom loves Egyptian history and she named me after an Egyptian queen."

"Wasn't one of Nefertiti's daughters named Meritaten?"

Justin asked, pleased that he remembered that bit of history from Nate's tour of the museum.

"That's right," Mrs. Bronson broke in. "I'm impressed with your knowledge, Justin. Meritaten was married to one of the pharaohs that succeeded Akhenaton."

Justin took a sip of his wine and relaxed. This wasn't going to be half-bad. While the rest of the group visited, Justin studied Merit. She had dark hair falling straight over her shoulders, a creamy light-tan complexion, a full mouth, and warm brown eyes. When she smiled, a dimple appeared on her left cheek.

"Have you been to Luxor yet?" she asked.

"No. But I hope to get down there next week." Justin quickly looked at his father to see if he had heard.

"You'll love it," Merit said enthusiastically.

"Where?" Justin's father interrupted.

"We're talking about Luxor. You know, where the Valley of the Kings is located," Justin answered quickly, and then added, "Nate has invited me to go down to see Luxor, Aswan, and the Temple at Abu Simbel with him. If it's all right with you, that is." He spoke the final sentence almost as a challenge.

"Well, now, I'm not so sure I want my son traipsing all up and down Egypt," Mr. Sanders began. But a nudge from his wife, accompanied by a warning look, made him add, "We'll talk about it later."

Just then, the waiter appeared carrying flaming shish-ka-bobs. Merit's eyes were shining as she said, "This is absolutely my favorite food!"

The conversation at the table lessened as they all concentrated on their food. Between courses, Justin and Merit silently enjoyed the spectacular view from the window. Cairo looked like a city out of the Arabian Nights, with orange lights glowing along the Nile and up and down the major highways.

As they were finishing their dessert of chilled cream puffs

covered with Swiss chocolate, they noticed a commotion at the entrance to the restaurant.

"Oh look!" Merit said."A bridal party!"

The band had been playing Western music—some fox trot, some rock—but it now changed to music with an Oriental sound. As the bride and her party walked to their tables, the band played "Here Comes the Bride" with an Oriental twang and beat.

Mrs. Bronson said, "It's the custom here in Egypt for a bride to be taken to see a belly dancer on the day she's married. That means we'll be able to enjoy the show too."

"Terrific!" Mr. Sanders gave Mr. Bronson a sly wink.

Justin hoped that Merit hadn't seen his dad's wink. He glanced quickly at her and found her completely engrossed by the beautiful bride and her party.

Before long, the belly dancer appeared. She was beautiful too, but a little too plump for Justin's taste. She was dressed in flowing layers of different colored chiffon, and of course, her belly was bare. Justin wondered again at the customs of this strange country when he saw men tucking money into the top of her costume as she danced near them. The men sure had everything their way here.

When the dancer had finished, the audience applauded generously, and the band resumed playing Western music again. Justin turned to Merit and met her smiling brown eyes. He had enjoyed her company much more than he had expected to. She wasn't giggly like so many girls in his class at school, and she loved Egypt and its history. All in all, it had been a great night. He was even regretful when the Bronsons suggested they call it an evening.

CHAPTER
7

 THE NEXT MORNING AT 6:30, JUSTIN WAS IN HIS BED, curled up in a tight ball. He was trying to go back to sleep, but his mind was churning out good, sound reasons that he could use to convince his father to allow him to go on the trip with Nate:

"It will be educational." (No. He already knows that.)

"We'll be safe. Nate knows his way around." (Maybe.)

"Nate's dad is letting him go." (No. Too whiney, kiddish.)

"We'll be scuba diving." (He'd like that.)

Just then the door to his room opened, and Justin's father looked in. Justin opened the conversation warily. "You're up early."

"I have a tennis match at seven o'clock. It's too damn hot to play any later than that."

Mr. Sanders walked to the window and looked down at the streets, already bustling with activity.

"Your mother and I had a long talk about you last night. She finally convinced me that you are capable of going on this trip."

Justin started to interrupt joyfully, but Mr. Sanders continued, "It's not that I don't trust you, Son. It's just that you're all we have, and I don't want anything to happen to you. You know, it's not easy for me to understand why you're so wrapped up in ancient history and that sort of thing. I'd like it if you were more interested in the same things that interest me. But I guess that's not in the cards. Anyway..." He spread his hands in a gesture of resignation. "Your mother tells me I'm not allowing you to grow up to be yourself. Maybe she's right."

Mr. Sanders turned from the window and looked at his son, his forehead wrinkled with concern.

"Oh, Dad." Justin was touched and embarrassed by his father's words. "I won't let you down, Dad. And—thanks. Thanks a lot for trusting me."

There was an awkward silence, and finally Justin said, "Would you help me make a list of supplies for scuba diving?"

"Scuba diving! Where on earth will you be doing that?" Mr. Sander's face broke into a broad grin. Temples and museums were one thing, but scuba diving was something else.

"I'm not quite sure just where, but it will be somewhere in Lake Nasser. You know, Dad, the lake that was created by the High Dam at Aswan. I think we're going to look at some flooded statues or something. Nate's the one who wants to do it. I'm going to teach him."

"Okay, Son. You make out the list, and I'll go over it. I'll also find out where the best place is to rent the stuff. Between the two of us, you and Nate will be all rigged out by noon."

After Mr. Sanders left, Justin called Nate immediately to tell him the good news.

"Come on up," Nate invited. "We can work on our supply

list and make plans for the trip."

"Be right there!"

As Justin started dressing, he thought back to the time when his dad had insisted he learn scuba diving. The family was on vacation in the Caribbean, and Mr. Sanders had become fanatically interested in scuba diving, as he was in so many other sports. Justin took the diving lessons reluctantly, only to please his father. About the third day, however, he found he was really enjoying the sport and was actually very good at it. It turned out to be one of the best vacations Justin had ever had, and it created a bond between his father and him that they both enjoyed. That had been three years ago, and since then they had gone scuba diving whenever they could.

Because of his knowledge of scuba diving, Justin felt pleasantly superior to Nate for the first time. He could hardly wait to teach Nate to dive. Justin knew he was good, and he was sure he could teach Nate all he needed to know.

The first thing Nate said when Justin entered the suite was, "What do you think? Can you teach me? Will I be able to learn?"

Justin laughed and said, "I'm absolutely sure, Nate—and I'm also super glad to be able to show you how to do something. These last few days you have completely shattered my ego. This afternoon we'll get the equipment, and tomorrow we'll start. Have you got some paper? I need to make a list."

Nate went to the desk, pulled out a sheet of paper, picked up a pen, and handed them to Justin.

"Okay, Professor, get started!"

Justin started writing, his face contorted with the effort of trying to remember everything they could possibly need. He could always shorten the list, but he didn't want to forget anything essential. Eventually, he paused and looked at his friend as he asked, "How serious are you about this? I mean, what, exactly, are you planning? Where are we going to dive? Do you want to dive deep? You know, the pool here at the hotel is only nine feet deep."

Nate, who had been studying a map, looked up and said, "We're going down to a place on Lake Nasser south of Abu Simbel. I understand that the water level in that area has risen about fifty feet, so I want to be able to dive to that depth and to stay down as long as possible. If it's all right with you, I'd like to camp out while we're there. I've never done it before, and I'd like to try it. What do you think?"

Justin looked up from his lengthening list and shook his head. Nate was really full of surprises.

It was later that night, just before he fell asleep, that Justin realized Nate hadn't told him *why* he wanted to dive in Lake Nasser. They'd been so busy all day getting their gear together he'd forgotten all about asking him again just what they were doing, and why. Justin smiled as he thought of the great help his father had been in teaching Nate the ropes of diving that afternoon. He had to admit, Nate caught on real fast.

Tomorrow, they'd practice some more in the pool, and then —the next day, Tuesday, they'd take off. He could hardly wait.

Early Tuesday morning, the boys with all their equipment were the first ones on the hotel bus that would take them to the airport. Mrs. Sanders, who had risen early to see them off, stood on the hotel verandah looking at the piece of paper Nate had handed her as they got on the bus.

Tuesday, June 19 - Old Winter Palace at Luxor
Wednesday, June 20 - Airport at Abu Simbel
Thursday, June 21 - Airport at Abu Simbel
Friday, June 22 - Return to Cairo.

What a considerate young man, she thought as she studied the brief itinerary.

The bus was only partially filled as it pulled away from

the hotel. It was a sharp contrast to the city buses crammed with humanity. On the ride to the airport, the boys were quiet, both lost in their own thoughts: Nate, hoping this search would be fruitful; Justin, thinking about his father and how helpful he'd been.

Then Nate interrupted Justin's thoughts. "Look, over there on your right. That's the City of the Dead."

Justin looked out at acres and acres of concrete buildings of all sizes. "It looks like a city with no lawns," he remarked.

"It's a cemetery," Nate explained. "But thousands of people live there, too."

"You're kidding!" Justin was incredulous.

"No, I'm not. Some are caretakers for the tombs of wealthy families, but most just make their homes in the different mausoleums. They even have a school for the children."

Justin shook his head in disbelief.

When the bus arrived at the airport, the two boys gathered their belongings together and stepped out into the hot sunshine and the bustling crowd. Unlike downtown Cairo, where men wore western-style clothes as well as traditional Egyptian robes, the airport was full of travelers dressed in flowing robes. Also conspicuous were large numbers of uniformed men— soldiers, policemen, airport officials—all carrying side arms.

"It's a good thing we got here early," Nate observed. "It'll probably take at least an hour to get on board."

"Why is that?" Justin asked.

"Because they examine all the luggage very carefully, and they frisk all the passengers," Nate replied.

There was one line for men passengers and another for women. The boys waited patiently, and when it was their turn, they found they had to explain about the scuba equipment to an airport official in another part of the building. As a result, they were the last ones to climb aboard the Egyptair jet. The plane wasn't crowded, so they were able to sit together. Nate insisted that Justin take the window seat.

"You won't ever really understand Egypt until you've seen the Nile River Valley from the air," he explained. "Then you'll know what they mean when they say Egypt is the Nile and the Nile is Egypt."

Airborne at last, Justin looked down and saw the city of Cairo completely surrounded by desert. He could see the many canals from the Nile that kept the city green. As they flew south, Justin understood what Nate meant about the importance of the Nile. The Nile River Valley was a narrow ribbon of green, anywhere from five to twelve miles wide, stretching through the unrelenting desert. On either side of the valley, for as far as he could see, there was nothing but sand.

"Impressive, isn't it?" Nate leaned over to look out the window too, and they both watched the river unwinding beneath them.

"Would you like some orange juice?" the steward asked, offering them a tray filled with paper cups.

"Thank you, yes." Nate handed a cup to Justin and took one himself.

"We'll be in Luxor soon," Nate said as he studied his watch. "I think we'll visit the Valley of the Kings this afternoon. You'd like to see King Tut's tomb, wouldn't you?"

"I sure would. But won't it be too hot to go in the afternoon?" Justin asked.

"Oh, it will be hot," Nate replied. "But the tombs are cool, and besides, there won't be as many tourists at that time of the day."

That settled, the boys obeyed the "fasten your seat belt" signs that had just come on. As the plane taxied to a stop, Justin peered out the window at the small airport shimmering in waves of heat. The dry heat took away their breath when they stepped out onto the landing steps.

"I thought it was hot in Cairo," Justin gasped. "I wonder what the temperature is here?"

"I'd guess about 112 Fahrenheit," Nate replied as he broke into a run. "Come on. I see an empty cab."

Running with all their gear in the intense heat was hard work. When they got to the cab, Nate asked breathlessly, "How much to the Old Winter Palace?"

"Five pounds, sir," answered the driver.

"Five pounds!" sputtered Nate, switching into Arabic. "It's not worth twenty-five piasters."

"Twenty-five piasters! That's an insult. What about my poor family? Three pounds!"

The driver seemed to be enjoying the bargaining, and so did Nate. They finally settled for a pound and a half.

"I could have gotten him down to a pound," Nate said regretfully, "only I didn't want to stay here all day."

During the hot, dusty drive into Luxor, Nate told Justin a little about the city.

"This area was called Thebes in ancient times. For thousands of years, it was the most important city in Egypt, but it had special connections with the Eighteenth Dynasty. Akhenaton and Nefertiti ruled from here before they moved the capital to Amarna. The boy-king, Tutankhamon, returned the throne to Thebes when he became pharaoh."

Nate ended the lecture when their cab pulled into the circular drive of a magnificent old hotel and stopped in front of a double flight of stairs rising to a broad porch. As Nate settled with their driver, Justin walked through a crowd of peddlers, some selling cheap jewelry, others, alabaster scarabs and small statues of Nefertiti. There were horse-drawn carriages everywhere, and their drivers pulled on Justin's arm, offering their services. Justin shrugged them off and hurried up the steps. At the top he turned and saw across the street the bright waters of the Nile. On the other side of the river was a small mountain range, shimmering in the heat.

Nate joined him and said, "Behind those hills is the Valley of the Kings, where King Tut was buried."

While Nate was registering and getting their key, Justin walked around the large lobby. There were inviting clusters of furniture all over the room. He looked up and saw that the ceiling soared several stories over his head. When Justin returned to the lobby after exploring the hotel dining room, he saw Nate struggling with their gear and looking for him.

"Here, let me help." Justin ran forward and took some of the equipment. "What's our room number?" he asked.

"We're lucky," Nate replied. "It's #234, just up those few stairs there and the second door on the right."

When they got to their room, Justin was surprised to find that the door had no lock. Just beyond it was a second, locked door, which led into the room itself.

Nate explained. "These doors are called 'Swiss Style.' Because we're close to the lobby here, they use the double doors to insulate against noise."

"Clever," Justin remarked.

They entered the darkened room, and Justin walked directly to the tall shuttered windows. He opened them and looked out at a beautiful garden with a swimming pool off in the distance. Next he turned his attention to the big, spacious bathroom.

"My God!" he called out. "What's this?"

Nate came in and saw Justin studying a piece of plumbing that looked like a urinal, except that it had a faucet inside.

"That's a foot bath." Nate was laughing as he said, "I didn't know what it was either the first time I was here. When we get back from the Valley of the Kings, you'll find out why they have these things."

Justin headed for a big comfortable arm chair and flopped down, hands behind his head. "What a neat place!"

"Don't get too comfortable," Nate warned. "We're going to have something to eat just as soon as we wash up, and then, we're off to see the Valley of the Kings."

CHAPTER
8

AFTER A LUNCH OF SOUP, CHEESE SANDWICHES, AND watermelon in the hotel dining room, the boys were ready to begin their exploring. When they walked out once again into the fierce Egyptian heat, they were immediately assailed by carriage drivers and sailboat operators looking for passengers. Nate shoved knowingly past them and led Justin down to the Nile, where a ferry was about to take off.

As they climbed aboard, Justin exclaimed. "It's almost empty!"

"That's why I wanted to go in the afternoon," Nate explained. "Luxor used to be a mecca for tourists only in the winter, but now it's popular all year round."

The trip across the Nile took only a few minutes. Once on the west bank, Nate began bargaining with yet another cab driver. The price finally agreed upon, the boys climbed in and settled back for the ride to the Valley of the Kings.

"We're going directly to the tombs," Nate said. "On the way back we'll stop and see the statues of Amenhotep III and Queen Hatshepsut's temple."

As they drove into the hills, curving up and around to the other side, Justin asked, "What are all those holes in the sides of the hill? Do people live there?"

"No," Nate replied. "They're all tombs. Remember, in ancient Egypt all the people were concerned with death and the afterlife, not just the pharaohs. Even the poorest wanted to be mummified and placed in a tomb. Archaeologists have found out a lot about what life was like for the ordinary people of those days from what they've uncovered in these small tombs."

They turned a corner, and the taxi slowed down near a large government building with shaded porches. When the boys got out of the cab, Justin started up the steps of the building, toward the inviting coolness he could see inside.

"Not yet!" Nate said as he grabbed Justin's arm. "We'll go there later. First, I want to take you into the tomb of Ramses VI, one of the pharaohs of the Twentieth Dynasty. His tomb was built almost on top of Tutankhamon's. Its being there is probably the main reason that Tut's tomb wasn't broken into and robbed like all the others."

A gatekeeper dressed in a flowing white gallabeo opened the gate to the tomb for them after Nate had pressed ten piasters into his hand. With sweat pouring down his face, Justin looked enviously at the gatekeeper's loose robe. "Those robes make a lot of sense in this heat. I wish I was wearing one right now."

As soon as they entered the tomb, it became much cooler. Relieved, they hurried down the ramp leading deep inside.

"It's huge," Justin said breathlessly, looking into the many small, beautifully decorated rooms on either side of the corridor.

Nate kept Justin firmly by his side as he pressed onward, deeper into the tomb. They finally came to an enormous room. In the center of it was the shattered granite sarcophagus of Ramses VI.

"I wanted you to see this tomb first," explained Nate. "The size and the decorations are typical of most of the pharaoh's tombs, and this one is particularly well preserved." He pointed at the walls. "Those drawings depict the exploits of Ramses VI. Up there, on your right. See the solar boats?"

"The colors are so bright," Justin noticed. "Have they been retouched?"

"No. They're the same as they were 3,000 years ago. To this day, no one knows the secrets of the Egyptian dyes."

Justin pointed at the ceiling. "Are those supposed to be stars?"

Nate looked up at the rock ceiling, which was painted dark blue and covered from side to side with gold dots. "Yes. Astronomy was very important to the ancient Egyptians, and of course they believed that when people died, their spirits went to the heavens."

The two boys walked all around the tomb, inspecting the smaller rooms. Justin had a hundred questions, and Nate had most of the answers. Finally, he said, "Now you're ready to see King Tut's tomb."

The climb out of the tomb was harder since it was all uphill. Justin could sense the heat as they approached the entrance. They were both temporarily blinded by the bright daylight as they emerged from the tomb. Justin thought longingly of a cold drink at the government house, but Nate was insistent.

The entrance to King Tut's tomb was far more elaborate than the one to Ramses' tomb. There was a gatekeeper here, too, who asked them if they had any cameras on them. Justin reluctantly handed his over before being allowed in.

What a surprise when they went into the tomb. "Why, it's tiny!" exclaimed Justin.

"That's why I wanted you to see Ramses' tomb first, so you'd have some idea of what a proper pharaoh's tomb should look like."

"But it's really beautiful," added Justin, as they walked into the coolness.

"Yes, isn't it?" Nate replied. "This tomb and the treasures found in it are typical of the art that flowered during Akhenaton and Nefertiti's reign. The art of the Amarna period. Almost everything that they did—the city they built, the temples—it was all destroyed by the pharaohs who followed them. They called Akhenaton the Heretic King because he tried to introduce a new religion. His successors wanted to wipe out every sign that he had ever existed."

Justin glanced quickly at Nate. He sounded so sad. Almost as if it had just happened, instead of being ancient history.

"Well anyway, the tomb has survived," Justin said, hoping to make Nate feel better.

But Nate solemnly shook his head as he said, "It's just not fair. One small tomb and a few other pieces are all that's left of the greatest art Egypt ever knew. It's not fair."

Suddenly, Nate realized that he was disturbing Justin. "I'm sorry," he said. "I don't know what came over me. I felt the same way when I was here with Father last winter."

By now the boys had reached the largest of the tomb's three rooms, the burial chamber itself. It was quite small but very beautiful, and it contained a great treasure—King Tut's mummy inside a gold-plated mummy case.

There was a small stairway leading to a stand overlooking the mummy case. The stand looked just like a pulpit, Justin thought, as he climbed up to it. The mummy case, protected by glass, gleamed with sheets of beaten gold. Within it was the boy-king's mummified body. On the wall just behind the case was a brilliant painting.

Nate explained the scene. "On the left is Osiris, God of the Dead, welcoming Tutankhamon, who is followed by his spirit double. In the center, Tutankhamon is shown standing before the sky goddess, Nut. On the right is Aye, King Tut's successor, performing a ceremony called 'Opening the Mouth' on King Tut's mummy. See, Aye is wearing the crown of Egypt, which means he is a king. He's also wearing a leopard skin, the sign of the priesthood. Aye was about eighty-five years old when this was painted."

"Eighty-five!" Justin exclaimed. "Why, he looks much younger. I thought you told me, or maybe I read it somewhere, that this art was supposed to be so realistic."

"It is. Look at his fat stomach. That is probably exactly how he looked," Nate said.

Justin leaned forward to study the image of Aye more closely. "He reminds me of someone."

Just then, Nate grabbed Justin's arm and started pulling him away. "Come on. We've seen enough. Let's get something cold to drink."

Justin backed away, still studying Aye. He finally turned and caught up with Nate.

Being prepared didn't ease the shock of the heat as they left the tomb and crossed the street to the government house. There was no air conditioning inside the building, but there were fans moving the air around. Although the temperature was in the nineties, it felt luxuriously cool by comparison with the sun-drenched sand and rocks outside.

Justin was deep in thought as he sipped a glass of cool grapefruit juice. Then suddenly he said, "I know who Aye reminds me of. Your father!"

"Justin, you're crazy!" Nate ridiculed the idea. "The heat's gone to your head."

"I know it's preposterous, but there *is* a resemblance." Justin wasn't about to give up his theory.

"Okay. Have it your way." Nate seemed to want to drop the whole conversation.

"Are we going to see any more tombs this afternoon?" Justin asked.

"I think you've seen enough. We're only going to be here this afternoon and tonight, and I want to show you some other things. Come on. The cab's right out front." Nate was on his feet, impatient to leave, but Justin paused on the way out to buy some slides of the inside of King Tut's tomb.

On the way back to Luxor they stopped briefly at Queen Hatshepsut's beautiful temple, with its terraces and colonnades. Justin enjoyed seeing the carved images of the female pharaoh dressed in men's clothing and wearing the false beard that was the symbol of Egyptian royalty.

They stopped again at the monolithic statues erected by Akhenaton's father, Amenhotep III. As they walked around the huge figures of the pharaoh and his twin self, Nate told Justin how in ancient times they came to be called the Singing Statues.

"They were probably damaged in an earthquake, and at times, when the wind was right, it sounded just as if they were singing. They stopped singing in 199 A.D.," he said regretfully, "when a Roman emperor had the damage repaired."

Justin took pictures of the statues from all sides, while Nate watched.

"Don't you have a camera?" Justin asked.

"My father and I did all that when we were here before," Nate explained.

When they finally returned to the river, the ferry had

just arrived and dumped a full load of tourists.

"See why I wanted to come here when we did?" Nate was pleased with himself for having avoided the crush.

"I sure do," Justin said appreciatively.

Back in their room at the hotel, Nate showed Justin how to use the foot bath to wash his sandy, dirty feet. Then, after a cool shower, they put on their swim trunks and went out to test the pool. The water was warm, but it was still fun.

"The dining room doesn't open till nine o'clock," Nate said as they left the pool on their way back to their room. "We have time to go see the great temples before dinner, and if you want, we can stop at the market on our way back."

The boys took a horse-drawn carriage the mile or so to the Temple of Karnak. Their driver was a young man named Ali.

"Do you want to buy a gallabeo?" Ali asked them. "My uncle has a shop in the market. I can get you a good price there. Very cheap."

"He'd get a commission on everything we bought," Nate whispered knowingly to Justin. "We can do much better on our own."

The Temple of Karnak was impressive, but the boys were tired and subdued. They wandered through the forest of enormous pillars, looking up at the bright blue of the late afternoon sky. Justin asked a few questions, which Nate answered, but neither boy's heart was in sightseeing.

When they left the temple, they found Ali and his carriage waiting for them. He was feeding his tired-looking horse some of the grass he carried in the front of the buggy. "You want to go to the market now?" he asked.

"Right!" Nate said, as he climbed aboard.

The carriage left the beautiful, broad street facing the Nile and entered a maze of narrow lanes clogged with donkeys, carts, and people. There were shops everywhere, selling all kinds of goods, and the smell in the air was powerful.

Because they were tired, Nate relented and allowed Ali to take them to his uncle's shop. When they got out of the carriage, they saw gallabeos of all sizes and colors hanging out in front of the shop. Inside the tiny room, the walls were covered from floor to ceiling with bolts of Egyptian cotton. Ali introduced Nate and Justin to his uncle, who sent his young son, a deaf-mute, out for some tea.

After being seated on two stools—produced, it seemed, out of thin air—the boys were shown the merchandise.

"I want one just like Ali's wearing," Justin said, pointing to the driver's plain blue (and very dirty) robe.

Ali's uncle reluctantly put away the elaborately decorated robe he had selected and pulled out a robe very similar to the one Ali had on, but clean.

"That's perfect. Let me try it on." Justin pulled the robe over his head and turned to Nate. "How do I look?" he asked.

"Like a real Egyptian," Nate laughed, and added, "except for the blue eyes."

Ali jumped up and, pointing to his own eyes, said, "Look at mine. They're green. And I have a cousin with blue eyes."

Just then, the little deaf-mute returned with a tray full of small glasses of hot tea. He twirled his finger at Justin as he offered him the tray.

"He wants to know if you like sugar in it," Ali explained.

Justin nodded his head, and the boy picked out a glass and handed it to him.

"Mmmm. This is good. Thank you," Justin said appreciatively.

Nate accepted a glass and drank the tea quickly. Then he said to the shop owner, "We'll take two of the gallabeos, and I won't pay a piaster over two pounds."

"Oh sir, these are the finest quality," the owner objected.

"Good Egyptian cotton. I can't accept less than ten pounds each."

Nate switched to Arabic, and Justin sat back, sipping his tea and enjoying the give and take of the bargaining. They finally agreed on three and a half pounds each, and while the robes were being wrapped in newspapers, Justin fished out his wallet.

"Let me buy these," he said. "You've been paying for everything." He waved Nate out of the way.

Later, back at the hotel, they decided to wear their gallabeos to dinner. The dining room was crowded, but the boys found a small table for two in the corner. Nate ordered a salad of the tiny Egyptian eggs, hard-boiled and sprinkled with herbs, a main course of veal, potatoes, and carrots, and chocolate sherbet for dessert. After studying the menu for a few seconds, Justin ordered exactly the same thing. He was too hungry to waste time choosing something else.

Midway through the meal, Justin took a sip of his mineral water and said to Nate, "Now. Can you tell me what it is we'll be looking for tomorrow? I assume that whatever it is, is under water. But just what is it?"

Nate did not answer but kept eating, slowly and deliberately. When they were finished with the main course and were waiting for the sherbet to be served, he finally answered.

"We're looking for a tomb."

"A tomb? You mean one that's never been found before? Not even by robbers or archaeologists?" Justin was intrigued.

"Yes." Nate's reply was brief.

"Whose tomb? And why so far south? Why not here at the Valley of the Kings where all the other tombs are?" Justin persisted.

"If you'll stop asking so many questions, I'll try to explain," Nate said. "Remember King Tut's tomb? How small it is compared to the tomb of Ramses VI? Most Egyptologists, including my father, believe that King Tut died suddenly and unexpectedly and there was no royal tomb ready for him. He had been pharaoh for such a short time that his tomb hadn't been finished yet."

"So whose tomb was he buried in?" Justin asked.

"We think that Tut was buried in a tomb that had been prepared for Aye," Nate replied.

"You mean that man whose picture is on the wall with King Tut? The one who I thought looked like your dad?" Justin was puzzled.

"That's right," Nate replied. "I told you before that my father and I believe Aye was the man behind the scenes during the reigns of several of the Eighteenth Dynasty pharaohs. Then he finally became pharaoh himself after Tut died. Aye was an extremely clever man." Nate was warming to the subject. "He was an artist, an architect, a physician, a philosopher... and he was probably the person most responsible for the beautiful art during Akhenaton and Nefertiti's reign." Nate added thoughtfully, "I believe that he may have been responsible for the change in religion, too."

Justin interrupted. "Let's get back to the question of the tomb. You're saying that Tut was buried in a tomb prepared for Aye. And Aye's real tomb has never been found?"

"There is a tomb in the Valley of the Kings that has been identified as Aye's. That is, his name appears on the walls. But my father and I, as well as some other archaeologists, don't believe that Aye was ever buried in it. We think that there is another tomb well hidden somewhere else. That's what we'll be looking for tomorrow in the area south of Abu Simbel."

"Incredible," Justin exclaimed. Then he asked, "But what makes you think the tomb is way down there? That's over 200 miles from here."

Nate grinned as he said, "It's because of *you* that we're going to that area to search."

"Who, me? What did I do?"

Remember the image of the ibis that you saw on King Tut's game board at the museum? The figure that didn't appear on any of the other boards?"

"Yes."

"The ibis was an important sign for Egyptian scribes, and Aye was a scribe, in addition to everything else. That's one of the reasons I connected the drawing with him. When I enlarged the photographs of the game board as you suggested, I found a tiny map within the image of the ibis."

"A map!" Justin exclaimed. "How could a map have been drawn that small? The Egyptians didn't even have magnifying glasses, did they?"

"You'd be surprised what the craftsmen of ancient times could do, even with their primitive tools. But let me finish the story. I found something on the map. It was the figure of another ibis, very small but unmistakable. When I checked its location on an ancient map used during Aye's time, I discovered that the little ibis marked a spot on the west bank of the Nile, south of Abu Simbel and north of the Second Cataract. I think that Aye's tomb is there, covered by the waters of Lake Nasser."

"You *think* it's there, but you don't have any real evidence," Justin said skeptically.

"Nothing positive," Nate admitted, "but I have a very strong feeling that I'm right. Tomorrow we're going to try to prove my theory. But right now we have to get some sleep."

Justin realized he had been listening to Nate so intently that he had forgotten all about his chocolate sherbet, which had melted to a chocolate-colored puddle in his dish. All of a sudden, he felt bone-tired. It had been an exhausting but exciting day.

That night as Justin lay in bed, he thought about everything that Nate had told him. When he fell asleep, he dreamed, not of an Egyptian princess, but of a fabulous treasure hidden in a mysterious underwater tomb.

CHAPTER 9

 THE PLANE FROM LUXOR LANDED GENTLY AND EXPERTLY on the dusty airfield at Aswan.

"We have to change planes here in order to get down to Abu Simbel," Nate explained as they walked to the small, dirty airport building.

When they discovered there would be a two-hour delay before the next plane left for Abu Simbel, Nate ran off to find a taxi. After checking their gear at the desk, Justin went out into the blistering heat to join him.

"We'll be able to see the dam," Nate said excitedly. "That's one thing my father and I haven't seen yet."

Their driver assumed the role of guide, pointing out the sights in the area. As they neared the dam, he slowed down and said, "See that white sculpture? It is in the shape of a lotus flower, the symbol of Egypt. It was a gift from Russia to Egypt in honor of the cooperation between the two countries in building the Aswan Dam."

He told them they could photograph the sculpture, but they absolutely could not take any pictures of the dam. Because of its strategic importance, security was very tight.

The Aswan High Dam was impressive—huge and beautiful. Nate and Justin got out of the cab and felt the cool mist from the falling water on their faces. The guide pointed southward and proudly said, "See, the great Lake Nasser. It stretches for 300 miles along the Nile River Valley. It is the second largest artificial lake in the world."

They stood enjoying the coolness for several minutes. Then Nate looked at his watch and said, "We should be getting back to the airport soon."

The cab driver made excellent time, and they arrived at the airport with twenty minutes to spare. In the waiting room, the boys saw a group of tourists picking disinterestedly at the box lunches they had brought with them. Most of them ate little or nothing and then put the boxes into the waste baskets. Justin noticed that the many robed men who had been standing idly around the airport were now busy emptying the waste baskets as fast as the tourists put the lunch boxes into them.

"That's their dinner," Nate observed. "They're really poor."

"You'd think they'd lose their dignity doing that," Justin mused. "But they don't."

The flight from Aswan to Abu Simbel was short. Before landing the pilot flew the plane low over the temple so that the passengers could see it from the air.

"Magnificent!"

"Incredible!"

"Awesome!"

Justin listened as the passengers tried to express their reactions to what they were seeing. He was equally impressed, but the words seemed inadequate to contain his feelings.

At the airport, Nate suggested that Justin go with the group of chattering tourists to see the temple. "I've got several things I must do here," he said.

"What things?" Justin was upset that Nate couldn't go with him.

"Well, first, I have to get permission from the government to camp out. And, then, I have to rent a boat for us," he explained. Nate added, "You can show me the temple tonight by moonlight. I hope we'll be camped near it."

Reluctantly, Justin joined the tourists just boarding the bus. The guide who accompanied them had a microphone in his hand and was just saying, "What we are going to see in a few minutes is really the result of two incredible engineering feats. The first, of course, was the original building of the temple and the huge statues in front of it during the Nineteenth Dynasty, around 1250 B.C. The second took place 3,000 years later when the engineers of over sixty nations cooperated through UNESCO to move the entire temple to the top of the cliffs to save it from the rising waters of the river."

He paused for effect, and then continued.

"You'll find the reconstruction was so carefully done that the fallen head of one of the statues is lying at Ramses' feet just as it was before. The engineers even constructed a hill around the temple, so that it still looks as if it is standing in front of cliffs."

The bus pulled to a stop, and Justin and the other passengers quickly got off. They were parked on the other side of the man-made hill and had to walk down and around the side of it. When they turned the last corner, they halted to stare in silence at the four huge statues of Ramses II sitting majestically at the front of the temple. Just as the guide had said, the second statue was headless, with its huge head lying at its feet.

The temple had a modern gate at its entrance, which was guarded by a tall, stately Egyptian in a flowing gown. He was holding an unusual short staff that looked something like an oval and a cross combined. The guide gestured toward the staff and said, "This is a very special symbol here and all over Egypt. You will see it many times in wall carvings and cartouches, in all the tombs and temples. It is called an ankh, which means 'key to life.' "

Justin looked closely at the gatekeeper's ankh and then followed the guide inside the temple, where the air was much cooler. There were statues everywhere, and the rock walls were covered with hieroglyphics and carvings showing the exploits of Ramses II. The guide allowed them to wander around by themselves for a while, and Justin enjoyed this free time. He saw the ankh symbol repeated many times in the drawings and also many images of solar boats. Then the guide called for them to follow him once again, this time far back into the temple.

"This is the holiest part of the temple," the guide began. "Here we see that Ramses II has done the most audacious thing of all. He has deified himself. You see? He has had his own likeness carved into a seated statue, and there he is sitting at the side of three great gods."

The guide paused again, then continued in a hushed voice. "This whole temple is dedicated to the sun-god Re, and each morning the first rays of the rising sun touch the front entrance. But on two days of the year, the sun's rays extend the entire length of the temple and reach this tiny inner room. They fall directly on the seated Ramses, now a god. During Ramses' lifetime, those two auspicious days were his birthday and the anniversary of the day he became pharaoh."

The man standing next to Justin asked the guide, "Does that still happen now that the temple's been moved?"

The guide was waiting for this question. He smiled and replied, "Yes, sir. The engineers who moved it were just as accurate as the ancient engineers. Twice a year, in February and October, that phenomenon happens."

Justin separated himself from the rest of the group clustered around the guide. He found a low step to sit on and thought about what he had just seen and what Nate had told him last night. Ramses' temple was beautiful, and the way it had been moved to the top of the cliff was remarkable. But what about Aye's tomb? Suppose it was located somewhere nearby. Aye might have chosen this remote stretch of the river as the site of his tomb 200 years before Ramses II ruled Egypt. Ramses' famous temple had been saved from the rising Nile, but Aye's tomb, never discovered, might even now be hidden under the waters of Lake Nasser. It was possible...

Justin roused from his thoughts long enough to look up and see the group of tourists filing out of the temple. He ran to catch up with them. They were headed for a second temple a few hundred yards north of Ramses' temple. Justin rejoined the group just as the guide was saying, "This temple was built for Nefertari, wife of Ramses II. *Nefer* means beautiful. So, Nefertari means the 'beautiful Tari.' "

The guide led the way into the temple, past another door-keeper holding an ankh. Justin pressed a coin into the door-keeper's hand and entered. This temple was far smaller than Ramses' but very beautiful. On both sides were statues of Nefertari dressed as the goddess Hathor. The pharaoh's wife had a round face, and she wore her hair parted in the middle and flipped up on the ends, much like today's hairstyle.

The tourists laughed appreciatively when the guide commented, "Although Nefertari was Ramses' twenty-fourth wife, she was obviously his favorite."

When they left Nefertari's temple, Justin was the first one back on the bus. He was anxious to return and see if Nate had been able to rent a boat and get permission for them to camp.

Back at the airport, Justin saw Nate sitting in the shade on the steps leading into the lobby. He jumped up when the bus pulled in and ran out to meet Justin.

"Everything's taken care of," he said proudly. "I had trouble getting the permit to camp, but a call to my father took care of it."

"How about the boat?" Justin asked. "Did you get one?"

"Yes, I got one. It's down by the shore. I've packed all our gear in it, and I even had time to get some food," Nate said smugly.

Justin was suitably impressed. "It didn't seem like I was gone that long."

The boys jogged down to the shore and Justin got his first close-up look at a felucca, a type of sailboat used all up and down the Nile. It was larger than he had expected, and although it stank of fish, he could see there was plenty of room for all their gear.

"Can you sail this thing?" Justin asked.

"Of course," Nate replied. "I love sailing. Ever since we got here I've sailed on every kind of boat. I spent several weeks in Cairo learning how to sail a felucca, and if I do say so myself, I'm pretty good!"

Nate proved true to his word, and they were underway in a few minutes. As they approached the site of Abu Simbel, Justin speculated out loud, "I wonder which will be most impressive—seeing the temple from the air or from the water?"

A few minutes later he exclaimed, "Far out! From the water! Definitely from the water!"

Then Justin pointed to a strip of land jutting out into the river. "See that? It looks like there are trees there. It would be a great place to camp—if they let us."

Nate expertly turned the boat so it was headed straight for the spot Justin had indicated.

"We can camp anywhere we want to," he said, "and that looks perfect!"

After a supper of flat Egyptian bread, cheese, and fruit, the boys pitched their small two-man tent. Then they changed into their gallabeos and sat down to relax and to watch the spectacular sunset.

Nate got out a couple of bottles of the mild Egyptian beer called Stella and said, "A surprise for you, Justin. Your parents won't mind, will they? It's not very strong."

"No, they won't mind," Justin replied. "My dad shares a can of beer with me every time he wants to have a man-to-man talk."

"What kind of talk?" Nate asked.

"Oh, you know. About girls and the facts of life. Or maybe, what you're going to do with your future... stuff like that. Don't you and your dad ever have talks like that?"

"Not really," Nate answered. "I don't have that many choices anyway. Everything's already been decided."

"What do you mean, already decided?" Justin interrupted. "Your future? Even girls?"

Nate seemed to be regretting the way the conversation was going. He said slowly, "I guess ours is what you would call an old-fashioned family. It's already been decided what I'll study and," he added shyly, "even who I'll marry."

Justin was stunned and started to question Nate further, but Nate said firmly, "I don't want to talk about it, Justin. Just let it be."

Nothing more was said for several minutes. Justin was regretting his prying questions, and Nate was regretting his sharp answer. Finally Justin broke the awkward silence by telling Nate about his thoughts concerning Aye's tomb.

"But even if the tomb is hidden somewhere along the river, how could we possibly find the exact spot?" he asked. "And what would we do if we did find it?"

Nate replied, "That's a mystery we'll solve tomorrow. Come on, let's get out the sleeping bags. We have to get up very early. We've got a big day ahead of us."

Justin protested that he wasn't the least bit sleepy, but he went along with Nate and prepared for bed.

Later, as the moon shone down on the ancient statues of Ramses II, it also lit up a bright orange tent with two sleeping boys inside it.

CHAPTER
10

IT WAS STILL DARK OUTSIDE WHEN NATE REACHED OVER and shook Justin gently. Justin crawled deeper into his sleeping bag and mumbled crossly, "Leave me alone."

Nate shook Justin, harder this time, and said, "Come on! Wake up! We've got to get started."

Justin raised himself to his elbows and squinted through the darkness at Nate, who was pulling on his swim trunks. Finally, Justin's sleep-fogged brain cleared, and he remembered what they had to do today. "I'm awake, I'm awake," he said. "I'll be ready in a minute."

Justin shivered as he crept out of the small tent to find his trunks. While he dressed, Nate checked over the scuba equipment and then carefully repacked it in the felucca.

The eastern sky was perceptibly brighter when the boys pushed the boat away from the shore with the help of two long poles. When they reached the main channel of the river, Nate raised the felucca's broad triangular sail. A gentle wind from the north pushed the sailboat south, away from Abu Simbel and toward the Second Cataract of the Nile.

As they moved south, the river became gradually narrower and the cliffs on either side closer. Nate explained that they were approaching the end of Lake Nasser, near Egypt's southern border. Before long, Nate asked Justin to hold the tiller of the boat and then began rummaging in the waterproof pack he had brought with him. Justin watched as Nate pulled out a gadget about the size of a small calculator.

"What's that?" he asked.

"It's a special device that will help us find the tomb," Nate responded.

"But how does it work?" Justin persisted.

"You'll see. Now turn the boat so that we can sail as close as possible to the western bank. We're not far from the Second Cataract and the area marked on the map."

By now the sun had risen above the horizon, and the cliffs along the river were stained red by its light. Justin stared in awe as the felucca drew near the rugged western shore. Suddenly, he was aware that a strange sound had intruded on the quiet of the majestic scene. Against the background of the sail's gentle creaking, he could hear a mechanical beeping noise. It seemed to be coming from Nate's gadget!

Justin watched in amazement as Nate adjusted some dials on his device. Was it a kind of Geiger counter? As they moved slowly along, the beeping noise became gradually faster and louder. Finally, it became a continuous shrill noise that echoed in the early morning silence. Nate said excitedly, "Quick, drop the anchor here! This is where we have to dive."

"What—" Justin got only one word out of his mouth when Nate interrupted.

"Justin, please be patient. If what I expect to find is there, I'll be able to answer all your questions. But right now, there's no time to explain."

Justin shut his mouth, and both boys quickly donned their scuba equipment. Nate slipped easily into the water, and Justin followed.

As the two boys sank into the cool, murky water, Nate kept his eyes on a depth gauge strapped to his wrist. When they had descended to a certain level, he motioned for Justin to stop and then swam over to the cliff wall. Justin watched as Nate got a powerful underwater flashlight out of his pack and began examining the wall of rock that had once been above the surface of the water. His search continued for several minutes. What's he looking for, Justin wondered. Then Justin saw it at the same time that Nate did—in the beam of the flashlight, the faint outline of a familiar shape. The image of an ibis, carved on the rock wall!

While Justin stared in disbelief at the twelve-inch-wide figure, Nate reached into his pack and took out the beeping gadget that he had used before. He pushed a button on the gadget, at the same time touching the center of the ibis figure with his other hand. Like a huge door, a section of rock swung outward, revealing an ascending flight of stairs cut into the cliff behind it. Justin almost fainted with surprise.

When Nate started swimming slowly up the submerged flight of stairs, Justin, recovered by now, was right behind him. Presently, they reached a point above the water level of the river where they could stand and take off their face masks.

Justin was so excited all he could do was stutter. "What was that? How did…?"

Nate put his finger to his lips and said, "Just a little longer, my friend. Right now we have work to do. Come on."

Justin followed Nate up a second flight of stairs that took them high up inside the cliff. At the end of the stairs, they were again faced with a blank rock wall. Nate played the beam of the flashlight over the wall, but nothing could be seen. Then he said, "Help me, Justin. Run your fingers over the wall. If you feel anything unusual, let me know."

Justin started running his fingers gently over the wall on the right-hand side, while Nate was examining every square inch on the left-hand side with the aid of the flashlight.

The two boys were becoming discouraged after fifteen minutes had passed and they could still find nothing. Then Justin felt a faint ridge with his fingertips and called excitedly to Nate, "Bring the flashlight over here. I think I've found something!"

Nate hurried over and pointed the light at the spot Justin indicated. Looking closely, they saw a tiny ibis carved in the rock.

"I knew you'd find it!" Nate said excitedly. "Just like the game board in the museum." After giving Justin a quick hug, Nate took out his calculator-gadget. He started to hand the flashlight to Justin, then changed his mind and said, "When I push the button, you push, very gently, on the ibis."

The tension was terrible. Both boys were reluctant to take this final step.

At last Nate said, "Now."

As he pushed the button on his gadget, Justin pressed gently against the ibis. Just as at the entrance, the huge rock swung smoothly outward.

It was dark in the chamber. Nate pointed his flashlight inside, and Justin groaned.

"It's empty!" He was sick with disappointment.

"No it isn't," Nate said softly. "Look." He swung the flashlight to the center of the room. There on a rock slab was a small chest carved out of alabaster and decorated with painted figures.

Then Nate swung the light so it played over the walls. They were covered with what looked like hieroglyphics. Finally, the beam of light cut through the darkness on the far side of the room.

Justin drew in his breath when he saw what was there—a skeleton crouched in the corner, hands folded, a golden necklace around its neck.

"Uncle Aye," Nate whispered.

Justin stared at Nate, a thousand questions on his lips, but he remained silent as Nate wept quietly, his hands covering his face.

When Nate finally had his emotions under control, he handed a tiny camera to Justin.

"Please, no questions yet. I need your help. Take a picture of every part of the walls of this room. Start there by the entrance and work your way from left to right around the room. Don't worry about the light. It's a special camera with very sensitive film, so the light from the flashlight will be enough."

Justin did as he was told.

Nate was busy too. First of all, he went over to the skeleton and carefully removed the index finger of the right hand, wrapped it, and put it in a small waterproof sack. He then took the jewelry gently off the bones and put it in another bag.

Nate seemed reluctant to leave the skeleton, but finally he went to the center of the room and very carefully opened the lid of the alabaster chest. Inside were two rolls of papyrus and a device just like the one he had used to move the rocks. Nate took out another waterproof bag and placed the strange device and the papyrus rolls into it This accomplished, he closed the chest, brushed off his hands, and walked over to where Justin was working.

"I'm almost through," Justin said. "Just a few more shots."

"Fine. The air seems to be good, but we shouldn't stretch our luck by staying here too long," Nate said as he studied the writing on the wall.

"Can you read that?" Justin asked.

"No. It looks like Egyptian hieroglyphics to me. Father will be able to, though. That's why I wanted the pictures."

"There. I've finished!" Justin said triumphantly, as he handed the camera back to Nate.

Justin peered at the corner where the skeleton was once again hidden by shadows.

"Is that really Aye?" Then he remembered and added disbelievingly, "Your *Uncle* Aye?"

Nate looked at Justin, then away. He seemed to be weighing his answer very carefully. Finally he sighed and said, "Yes, it is Aye. And yes, it is my uncle."

"But that would be impossible! No one can have an uncle who lived over 3,000 years ago!"

Nate put his hand on his friend's shoulder and said, "Justin, we must leave now. I promise I'll tell you everything, answer all your questions, when we get back to the camp."

When they had placed the waterproof sacks containing the treasures in their two packs, the boys took one last look at the room. Nate let the light linger for a few seconds on the skeleton before he turned to leave.

"Aren't you going to reclose the wall?" Justin asked.

"No. I'm going to leave it open. I'll call Father this afternoon, and if he thinks it should be permanently closed again, we can come back and do it tomorrow."

They walked down the steps to the point where they had to put on their scuba gear again.

"We'll close the lower entrance most of the way, but we'll leave a small opening," Nate said before putting in his mouthpiece.

Justin nodded, and the two boys entered the water and started their swim down the stairs and out the entrance. When they finally got back to the camp several hours later, Nate asked Justin to be patient just a little longer while he went to the airport to call his father.

"You wait here. I won't be gone long. And please don't touch anything from the tomb until I come back," Nate said as he climbed again into the felucca.

Justin found a shady spot among the trees from which he could watch the unending stream of tourists who were coming to see the Temple of Abu Simbel. His mind was filled with the discovery they had made that day. Archaeologists could spend a lifetime digging and never come up with anything so great. He wanted the acclaim and attention that this discovery would bring him, but most of all, he wanted to hear Nate's story.

CHAPTER
11

WHEN NATE RETURNED FROM THE AIRPORT, HE FOUND Justin asleep in the shade, worn out from the adventures of the morning. Nate smiled down at his sleeping friend and then took from the tent the waterproof bags they had brought back from the secret cavern. Quickly, he opened the bag with the papyrus scrolls in it. He unrolled the first and skimmed over it. After a few minutes, he put down the first scroll and opened the other.

For the next hour, while Justin slept, Nate read. He noticed Justin stirring just as he finished.

"Are you hungry?" he called.

"Starving!" Justin replied.

Nate opened the cooler and took out the leftover bread, cheese, and fruit that would be their supper. "I hope this isn't stale," he said as he handed Justin's share to him.

"Even if it is, it won't matter. I'm so hungry I could eat a camel." Justin took a big bite of the bread and started chewing.

"How about building a fire when the sun goes down?" Nate suggested.

"A perfect setting for storytelling," Justin hinted.

Because they were so near the equator, the sun would set shortly after six o'clock, as it did every day. As the light faded, Justin gathered up twigs while Nate got some charcoal out of the felucca. Shortly, they had a small fire started. It was still too hot to sit near it, so they settled down several yards away.

"Now... ," said Justin.

Nate began. "First of all, you must promise me you'll never tell anyone about what has happened here."

Justin was dismayed. One of the greatest archaeological finds of the century and he could tell no one?

"That's not fair," he objected.

"Please. Hear me out, Justin," Nate implored. "I've talked with Father. He realizes the importance of the find and wants you to have credit for it. He also wants scholars to be able to study what is written on the walls of the cavern. It is almost certainly a complete history of Aye's time on earth, and it would be of great help to historians of the Eighteenth Dynasty."

Justin was relieved, but still puzzled. "Why are you being so mysterious then?" he asked.

Nate took a long time answering. Finally he said, "Father doesn't know you saw the device that opened the entrance. I let him think I was alone at the time I used it. But more importantly, he doesn't know that I slipped and called Aye my uncle!" Nate sighed, then added, "And he doesn't know that I'm going to tell you the whole story of our being here."

"I see," Justin said softly.

"You're the only real friend I've ever had," Nate continued, "and I want you to know about me. But please," he entreated, "please promise you'll never betray my confidence in you."

"I give you my promise, Nate. That's all I can do."

"That's enough for me," Nate answered.

When Nate finally began talking, he spoke so softly that Justin had to edge closer.

"Around 7,000 years ago, my people had an advanced society located on a small continent in what you call the Atlantic Ocean—a continent that no longer exists."

"Atlantis!" Justin exclaimed. "I knew it wasn't just a legend!"

Nate nodded and continued, "We were governed by a small group made up of scientists, philosophers, and artists. Our way of life was luxurious, thanks to our technology, and our people were happy. Then something happened. Late in what we called the Omega century, our astronomers discovered that an approaching meteor, the size of a small planet, was going to pass so near the earth that a shift in its axis was inevitable. Our geologists knew that the shift would cause earthquakes of an intensity never before witnessed, followed by a melting of the polar ice caps and a rise in ocean levels all over the world. It would mean annihilation of life as we knew it."

"So that's what happened to Atlantis!" Justin exclaimed and then said, "Go on."

"The leaders did not tell the people, because there was no way of saving them all. But efforts were begun to preserve some part of our civilization. One thing the leaders did was to encourage our more adventurous citizens to leave home and settle in parts of the world where, according to predictions, the coming devastation would be less severe."

Nate interrupted his tale to add, "In fact, Father and I have found evidence suggesting that people from our continent influenced the early Mayan and Incan cultures. They also left their mark in Mesopotamia and Egypt."

He paused for a breath, and then resumed.

"At the same time, our scientists began the construction of a space ship. Since the principle of anti-gravity had recently been discovered, the size of the ship could be immense. And it would have anti-matter engines for propulsion so it could travel great distances.

"The selection of the people who would escape on the ship was not left to individuals, who would have had a personal investment, but to a giant computer. The computer was pro-grammed with the requirements of a self-sufficient community that might have to wander in space for centuries. It was then fed the profiles, abilities, and personality characteristics of all the citizens of Atlantis. The computer alone made the choices, and many of those who worked hardest on the project were not selected."

"How sad," Justin couldn't keep from saying.

"My ancestors were among those selected. My grandfather Hotep was a boy of fifteen at the time. My grandmother Isis was ten years old and already a child prodigy in music. Each was summoned to the capital and told about the coming disaster and the space ship. They could have refused to take part in the project. If they had, all memory of the information they had received would have been hypnotically removed from their minds. However, they both consented."

"Lucky for you," Justin said.

"They were both put into a dormitory-school where they would receive the training necessary to make them functioning members of the crew. You see, there were to be no passengers on the ship—only crew members."

"What about their parents?" Justin asked.

"They knew nothing about the coming disaster," Nate explained, "but they were honored and pleased that their children had been selected for this special school. Grandmother continued her education in music. Her duty would be to keep music alive in the space community by performing and by teaching others. Grandfather was given intense training in astrophysics so that he could help with the ship's navigation."

Nate paused in his narrative. Justin, determined not to interrupt again, sat silently, waiting until Nate continued.

"Some of the scientists who had not been selected for the big ship, probably because of their age, used smaller anti-gravity ships to visit communities in remote parts of the earth. Each one gave a message to a respected and honored person in the community. The message was the same everywhere—in the Tigris-Euphrates Valley, in Mexico, Greece, North America —everywhere the messengers went, they confided in one person the fact that there would soon be a catastrophic flood."

"Noah!" Justin exclaimed.

"That's right," Nate smiled. "But there were many 'Noahs.' Each one was instructed to immediately start building a huge ship and to stock the ship with the plants and animals of their area, plus the stores necessary to keep them alive for several months.

"That's one of the exciting things that Father and I researched here in your great libraries." Nate's face was animated. "Do you realize there is a flood story existing in virtually all ancient cultures?"

Justin shook his head. "No, I didn't."

"Well, there is. And if my ancestors had not done what they did," Nate added proudly, "it's possible that life would have been wiped off the face of the earth."

After mentioning this grim possibility, Nate picked up the threads of his story.

"Eventually, the selection of the members of the space ship

was completed. Some of those chosen refused to believe that the apocalypse was really going to happen and decided against giving up their comfortable lives for the rigorous training necessary. Others didn't want to leave their families. All of these people were hypnotized and knowledge of the impending catastrophe wiped from their minds.

"The final population of the space ship was younger than the leaders had hoped for. However, all the crew members had been chosen for their ability to get along with each other, plus the unique functions they could offer the ship. Grandfather, in spite of his young age—remember, he was only fifteen—was a vital member of the crew. He would help chart the course the ship would take.

"You may find it hard to believe, Justin, but all of this took place only seventy years ago." Nate paused, then added, "Space-Ship Time, that is."

Justin, jolted out of his trance, began to protest and to demand an explanation. But he had to wait until after Nate had walked off into the brush to relieve himself. On his way back to the campfire, Nate crawled into the tent to get sweaters for Justin and himself. Despite the fire, the breeze off the river was becoming chilly.

Justin gratefully put on the extra sweater. He had been so engrossed in Nate's story that he hadn't noticed how uncomfortable he was. Now he waited impatiently while Nate put some more twigs on the dying embers and stirred them until yellow flames licked up toward the haze drifting in from the river.

Finally, to Justin's immense relief, Nate returned to the perplexing subject of Space-Ship Time. "Because the Atlantean space ship was powered by an anti-matter engine, it could travel at speeds approaching the speed of light." He paused, groping for the right words. "I don't know how much you know about this field..."

"Not much," Justin admitted. "I've always been more interested in history than in science."

"You have heard of Albert Einstein?" Nate asked.

"Of course!"

"Well," Nate continued, "about seventy years ago—in earth time, that is—Einstein re-discovered the theory of relativity."

"Re-discovered?"

"That's right. My people knew all about the principle of relativity. They knew that when an object like a space ship approached the speed of light, something happens to the passage of time. Everything aboard the ship, including clocks and people, slows down with respect to time on earth. Events seem to take place at a normal rate, even though years might go by on earth before a second elapses on the ship."

"I know what you're talking about!" Justin said excitedly. "My science teacher explained it by using the Twin Paradox of Relativity. Let's see if I can remember it." Justin wrinkled his forehead in concentration. "If one twin brother stayed on earth while the other flew to a star at nearly the speed of light..." He hesitated and then finished with a rush, "When the space-traveling twin returned, he'd be younger than the brother he left behind!"

"Exactly," said Nate. "And that's what has happened on the space ship from Atlantis. For every ten years spent in space, approximately one thousand years have passed on earth."

Justin whistled in astonishment, and Nate laughed. Then he cleared his throat. "I'm thirsty from all this talking. Let's have a bottle of beer while I take a rest."

The boys stood up and stretched to relieve their cramped muscles. Justin got two bottles out of the cooler and opened them. The beer was not cold but it felt good sliding down their dry throats.

"Why don't we sleep outside the tent tonight," Nate suggested. "Let's get into our sleeping bags now, before I go on with the story. We'll be warmer and more comfortable."

Justin poured water over the remains of the fire while Nate got the bags from the tent. A few minutes later, they were both stretched out, side by side, looking up at the stars in the black night sky.

CHAPTER 12

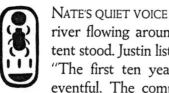 NATE'S QUIET VOICE BLENDED WITH THE SOUND OF THE river flowing around the point of land where their tent stood. Justin listened intently as his friend spoke. "The first ten years aboard the space ship were eventful. The computer had chosen wisely, but it was still up to the inhabitants to create a just society. A form of government had to be devised to administer and to allow the group to act as a unit. It was decided that the family was still the best foundation of a workable society but that a form of birth control through selection was necessary. Families were started with the aid of the computer, which matched likes and dislikes and personality traits along with genetic factors."

Nate interrupted his story to explain, "That's what I meant when I told you a girl had been selected for me. I know that sounds cold and indifferent, but I assure you, it's most necessary." Nate laughed. "When Father and I were in New York City, we saw computer-dating services offered in the newspapers. Believe me, there's nothing new under the sun!"

"All your ancestors were matched by the computer?"

"That's right. Grandfather Hotep and Grandmother Isis were selected for marriage when he was thirty and she was twenty-five. They had known each other for about fifteen years. They were permitted to have one child, but somehow the computer miscalculated, and they had twin sons: Ik, my father, and Aye, my uncle.

"When his sons were still quite young, Grandfather became the victim of an incredible longing for the earth. Against Grandmother's wishes, he petitioned to be allowed to return to his planet during the ship's next swing into the solar system." Nate paused.

"By now, the ship had been traveling for 20 space years, or 2,000 earth years. Ten years earlier, it had come into this solar system. At that time, two inhabitants of the ship had become so distressed at being close to their former home that they made an attempt to return to the earth. They didn't survive. The Elders, realizing that this situation was apt to repeat itself, started work on a small space 'boat' that could safely land a person on earth."

"Is that where the Egyptians got their idea about solar boats carrying the dead pharaohs through the heavens?" Justin asked.

"That's my theory. I'm going to ask Father if he's found anything to connect our space boats with the Egyptians' solar boats."

"I'm sorry I interrupted," Justin apologized. "Please, go on."

"Let's see. Where was I?"

"The space boats. The Elders were working on them."

"Yes. Well, they did succeed in building a small space boat, but they could not overcome the problem of how to make the home ship decelerate and remain in the solar system long enough for the small craft to return to it. Therefore, if Grandfather chose to leave the ship, he would have to spend the rest of his life on earth."

"Wow! What a decision!" Justin said sympathetically.

Nate nodded in agreement and continued. "He chose to go. The Elders believed that Grandfather should not be just a sightseer on earth but that he should help the people he met. So they saw to it that he had training in many fields—architecture, mathematics, astronomy. But most of his training was in medicine. The Elders felt that would be the most beneficial art he could take with him.

"After Grandfather left the home ship, he used the sophisticated equipment aboard his space boat to locate an area where civilization had developed. He came eventually to the fertile Nile Delta and saw the Great Pyramid of Giza. When he realized that the pyramid had been built by a visiting Atlantean before the flood, he decided to make that area his home."

"Aha," Justin said. "That's why you were so positive about which pyramid was the oldest."

"I was nearly positive," Nate replied. "It wasn't until I had read Grandfather's diary that I knew for sure."

"His diary?"

"Those papyrus rolls in the alabaster chest were Grandfather's and Uncle Aye's diaries. I skimmed through them while you were sleeping this afternoon."

"But I thought you couldn't read hieroglyphics."

"They weren't written in hieroglyphics. They're in my native language," Nate explained. "That's why they cannot be made public."

Noting Justin's puzzled expression, he added, "Let me finish. You'll understand why then.

"When Grandfather settled in Egypt, he quickly learned the language and customs of the area and took the name Imhotep. His knowledge and native intelligence brought him to the attention of the Pharaoh Zoser, and within a short time, he was chosen the pharaoh's Grand Vizier.

"The Grand Vizier Imhotep became a very influential man, and his accomplishments were many. He was best known for his contributions to medicine, but he was a great architect too."

"I remember!" Justin said. "He built the Step Pyramid. What's the story behind that?"

"It happened this way. The Great Pyramid at Giza was an object of worship to the people of Egypt in those days. Even the sea shells found in the corridors were considered holy. The Pharaoh Zoser was fascinated by the pyramid and wanted to build a monument like it for his tomb so that he too would be considered divine. Grandfather used his architectural training and his anti-gravity device to create the Step Pyramid."

"Did you find all that out from his diary?" Justin asked.

"Yes. It really helped fill in the gaps. I also learned that he married a Nubian woman and had a large family but that he never forgot his family in space. By using his Atlantean-taught skills of healing through meditation, Imhotep lived to be 135 years old! After his death, he was made a god. That's how great his impact on Egypt was."

Nate paused, deep in thought about this grandfather he had never known.

Finally Justin asked, "What was happening on the space ship while Imhotep was being made a god in Egypt?"

"The twins Aye and Ik were growing up, totally unaware of their father's accomplishments on earth. As they grew older, they both found the lure of earth to be all-consuming. When they were about twenty years old, they appealed to the Elders for the chance to return to earth together when their ship was once again in the solar system. The Elders, much to Grandmother's relief, decided that the colony could not afford to lose both of the boys. So they left it up to the twins to decide who would go, and who would remain. The boys settled the matter by playing their favorite board game, Senet. The winner would go, the loser would stay aboard the ship and father a child."

"Wait a minute!" Justin interrupted. "I'll bet that's the same game as the one in King Tut's tomb—right? That explains how you knew the rules to a game that my guidebook said were lost forever. I wondered about that."

"Aye won that game of Senet on the space ship," Nate said. "He was the dreamer of the two young men. Art, philosophy, and architecture were his main interests. My father was the practical realist. Science and engineering were his strong points, and history, his hobby.

"Aye's trip to earth was planned in great detail. The Elders wanted him to land near the place where Hotep, his father, had landed and to look for some evidence that Hotep had survived. Aye was given the same simple instructions that Grandfather had been given—'Do no harm.'

"According to his diary, Aye landed near Thebes. Only 12 space years had passed since his father had made his journey, but on earth it was 1,200 years later! Amenhotep III was pharaoh of Egypt. Remember him? He was Akhenaton's father, the ruler who expanded trade and helped make the Eighteenth Dynasty so great. After learning the language and customs of the people, Aye quickly became a trusted aid of the pharaoh and tutor to his children. He married the royal nurse Ayah, and they had many children of their own, among them the beautiful Nefertiti."

"Just think!" Justin broke in. "One of the most beautiful women in the history of the world was your cousin."

"I hadn't thought of that," Nate said reflectively. "I wish I could have known her." He continued his story.

"Aye didn't forget his mission of discovering what happened to his father. He had learned that among the many deities worshipped by the Egyptians was a god of healing called Imhotep, and he suspected that Imhotep and Hotep were one and the same. After searching for many years, following clues centuries old, Aye was led to his father's creation, the Step Pyramid. There, in a secret corridor deep underneath the pyramid, he found Hotep's diary. Grave robbing had become epidemic by this time, so Aye took the diary with the intention of hiding it in a safer place.

"Aye the philosopher was disturbed at the deification of his father. He knew that although Hotep was undoubtedly a great and gifted man, he was only human. Aye's concern about this eventually led him to make the greatest of all mistakes."

Nate's voice had fallen almost to a whisper, and Justin moved closer so he wouldn't miss a word.

"Aye wanted to lead the people away from their belief in many gods, which he felt was preventing the Egyptian civilization from becoming truly great. He wanted to see an end to the conflict between religious factions led by the priests who served the different gods. Aye believed that Egypt would have a better chance for lasting peace and prosperity if it were united by a belief in one God. So he began teaching his royal pupils the concept of a single, loving God.

"The child Amenhotep IV was an eager student. He was much like Aye—a poet, an artist, and a philosopher. When Amenhotep IV followed his father as pharaoh and married Aye's daughter Nefertiti, Aye believed that his most cherished dream would be realized through their reign.

"At first it seemed that Aye's plan had succeeded. After

Amenhotep became pharaoh, he changed his name to Akhenaton, thus announcing his belief in a single God, Aton, whose symbol was the disk of the sun. The pharaoh replaced the worship of Egypt's many gods with the worship of this one all-powerful God. He moved the capital from Thebes to a new city, which he called Akhetaton, the Horizon of Aton. Today we know it as Amarna. Under Aye's influence, Akhenaton ordered the architects to design a city with functional yet beautiful buildings; he commissioned artists to do realistic paintings and sculpture. For a few brief years, Aye's dream seemed to have come true."

"Why didn't it last?" Justin asked.

"According to his diary," Nate replied, "the priests of the god Amon were angry at losing their power and influence. And the common people were just not ready to give up the worship of their gods.

"Poor Aye," Nate sighed. "How he must have suffered during the last years of Akhenaton's reign. He came to realize that the Egyptians were not ready for the changes he had tried to make. Finally, he understood that he had unwittingly violated the Elders' command—he had done harm to the people he had come to help.

"But Aye realized his error too late. He lived to see his beloved daughter Nefertiti murdered, and his pupil Akhenaton hated and feared by the people of Egypt. After Akhenaton's death, Aye was instrumental in having Tutankhaton, Akhenaton's half-brother, made pharaoh at the young age of nine. Aye advised Tutankhaton to change his name to Tutankhamon to appease the priests of Amon. He also persuaded the young pharaoh to move the capital back to Thebes. But it was too late to undo the harm that had been done or to preserve any part of the new religion that Aye had worked to establish."

Nate's voice was husky with emotion as he described the last years of Aye's life.

"By the time Tutankhamon was pharaoh, Aye was in his late eighties, and his thoughts were often with his twin brother in space, who was only a few months older than when Aye had left him. He became obsessed with the idea of communicating with his twin and also with finding the perfect place where his own diary and his father's could safely weather the passage of time.

"His duties as Grand Vizier took him up and down the Nile, and it was on one of these pilgrimages that he found the right spot. The cliffs along the river are made of limestone, and they are honeycombed with natural caverns. Along the top of the cliffs in the area then known as Nubia, Aye discovered a small opening that led to a cavern within the cliff wall. He decided that it could be made into a perfect hiding place. So he had steps carved into the cliff, from the bank of the river up to the secret cavern. When the work was completed, he sealed both the lower and the upper entrances with huge rock doors that only he could move, marking them with the sign of the ibis.

"After Aye had made his hiding place secure, he returned to Thebes and gave his full attention to his duties as Tutankhamon's advisor. But the pharaoh's brief reign was already near its end."

"Does Aye's diary tell how Tutankhamon died?" Justin asked.

"He fell from his chariot," Nate replied, "and was in a coma for several weeks. Uncle Aye tried everything, but the brain damage was too extensive. When Tut died, he was buried in the tomb that Aye had been building for himself. Aye had already prepared the game board with the message on it, and he made sure that it was included among the treasures placed in the young pharaoh's tomb."

Both boys fell silent for a while, thinking about the boy-king and his untimely death. Then Nate continued.

"Aye reigned as pharaoh himself for a few years after Tutankhamon died. By now he was over 100 years old, and he sensed that his own end was near. He did not want to be buried in the royal tomb being prepared for him, nor did he want his body to be mummified. So at the end, Aye went alone to the secret cavern by the river. He reread his father's diary and finished his own. Then he waited for death to come."

Nate's voice died away, and there were a few minutes of silence. Then Justin spoke. "The writing on the walls of the cavern? Did Aye do that?"

"Yes," Nate answered. "He wanted the correct history of Akhenaton's time to be recorded somewhere. The priests of Amon had destroyed Amarna and all the temples and monuments that told of those brief years. Aye wanted to be sure that the true story would survive. Before he died, he was convinced that his twin, my father, would find the cavern and all the information it contained. The last entry in his diary was written to Ik:

Dearest Brother,
Your search has ended. All your questions are answered here. Take care that you do not repeat my mistake. DO NO HARM."

Nate stopped talking. Aye's story was finished.

CHAPTER
13

AYE'S STORY WAS FINISHED, BUT JUSTIN WASN'T SATISFIED. "I still don't get it," he said. "What harm did Aye do?"

"He introduced a new religion to a society that wasn't ready for it," Nate explained. "He tried to alter the course of history, and he ended up hurting a great many people. That's why you must never tell anyone about my father and me and what you've heard tonight."

"I still don't understand the secrecy," Justin persisted. "You're not introducing a new religion."

"If the truth about us and our civilization ever got out," Nate said patiently, "we'd be forced to share our technological advances with the people of the earth. And they just aren't ready to deal with such information—yet."

Justin started to protest, but Nate continued.

"Who would we give the anti-gravity device to? Or the principle of the anti-matter engine? The Egyptians? The Americans? The Russians? The United Nations? Can't you see the problems that would create?

"No." Nate shook his head and answered his own questions. "Our instructions were very clear. We were only to observe—never to interfere."

"Okay," Justin said regretfully. "I promised to keep your secret, and I won't break my promise. I swear." Then he added, "But what about you and your dad? Tell me how you came to be here."

Nate cleared his throat and took up his story once again.

"During the past ten years, the astrophysicists on the ship finally solved the problem of slowing the vessel down and putting it in orbit around the sun so that anyone who left the ship to visit the earth could return. My father and I were selected for the next earth mission because of our relationship to Hotep and Aye—and also, because Father is an historian. Our task would be to record the history of the earth since the flood, with special emphasis on documenting the impact of the previous one-way visitors from our ship.

"In preparation for our journey, we tuned in to the radio waves from earth so that we could learn as much as possible about your culture. We also learned to speak and read three languages: Arabic, English, and Chinese. We were given several false identities and the documents to support them so that we could visit different countries without attracting suspicion. And we were supplied with a large amount of gold—made on the space ship—which we would deposit in a Swiss bank and use to pay our expenses.

"Our travels during the last three years have taken us to all parts of the earth. We saw the Mayan ruins in Mexico and Central America. We concluded that the civilizaton was influenced by Atlanteans before the flood, but that there had been no visitors from our ship. We went to Stonehenge in

England and to Easter Island in the Pacific. We visited the Berlin Museum and saw the famous head of Nefertiti. The collection of the Field Museum in Chicago was very important, too. But Cairo and the Egyptian Museum were the most fruitful. We were awfully disappointed that the great library at Alexandria had been destroyed. And we were both surprised and dismayed to find that no real evidence of the existence of Atlantis had survived.

"And that brings us up to now," Nate concluded. "But you probably still have many questions."

"I sure do!" Justin exclaimed. "Where did you land? Where is your space boat now? When do you go back? How does that anti-gravity gadget work? Why did it make that beeping noise? How did—?"

Nate laughed and said, "One question at a time. Please. First of all, I can't tell you where we landed or anything about our craft. And that's final." Nate was emphatic about this, and Justin didn't argue.

"I *can* tell you when we return—we leave the earth next month," Nate said sadly. "I'll really miss the blue skies, the feel of the wind, sailing." Most of all, I'll miss you, Justin."

"Why don't you stay? You could live with us!" Justin said excitedly.

"That wouldn't be fair," Nate answered. "To Father, to Grandmother, or to the others on the ship."

Both boys lay silently, wrapped up in their own thoughts.

Then Nate said, "You asked about the anti-gravity device and the sound it makes. The device is equipped with a sensor that's activated by the presence of another anti-gravity device. I was sure that Aye's device would be in his tomb, and I was right. The sensor on my device began sending out signals when we got near the tomb. The closer we got, the stronger the signals became."

"So that's what was going on! But what about the anti-gravity part of the thing? How does it work?"

"I'm not an engineer, so I can't really explain how it works," Nate answered. "I just know that it does work and that it's one of the most important technological advances ever made by our people. Without it, our space ship could never have escaped from the earth. Anti-gravity equipment also protects us from being hit by space 'garbage' like meteorites."

"Boy! What a breakthrough it would be for the American space program if we had the anti-gravity device and the anti-matter engine," Justin said and then quickly added, "I know. I promised and I'll keep my promise, but..." His words trailed off.

"Look, Justin," Nate entreated. "We have proof from Uncle Aye's diary that his interference helped to bring down a whole dynasty. Just think what might happen if we revealed these secrets. Why, it could destroy the whole earth!"

"Or it could save it," Justin replied.

"That's the problem, my friend," Nate said conclusively. "We don't know. *We just don't know.*"

Nate looked seriously at Justin for a few seconds, and then he smiled. "No more questions, okay? We both have a lot to do tomorrow." He reached over and touched Justin's shoulder lightly. "Good night, good friend," he said.

Nate fell asleep almost immediately, but Justin lay awake for a while, staring at the stars. The last thing that crossed his mind before sleep came was the command of the Atlantean Elders, the principle that guided Nate's actions—DO NO HARM.

Justin was awakened by a tickling sensation caused by a drop of sweat running down his nose. He reached up to wipe away the sweat and opened his eyes to the perpetual Egyptian sun. Morning already. Then he remembered. It wasn't a dream. It had really happened!

Justin glanced over to where Nate had been sleeping and noticed that the bag and its occupant were gone.

He must be in the tent, he thought.

As he pulled himself slowly out of the hot sleeping bag, he called Nate's name.

No answer.

Zipping up his jeans, Justin went over and poked into the tent. There was no sign of Nate.

"Maybe he's in the boat." Puzzled, Justin walked down to where the felucca had been moored. It was gone! He looked back at the grove of trees, cupped his hands over his mouth, and called, "Nate? Where are you, Nate?"

Then he stopped and listened. Only silence.

"He's gone! But why?"

Justin checked the tent again and found that all of Nate's things were gone. He rummaged through the rest of the stuff.

Nothing.

It was after he crawled out of the tent that he finally saw it: an envelope, pinned to the front flap. Quickly he pulled it off, tearing the corner as he did so. When he ripped the envelope open, his return ticket to Cairo fluttered to the ground. With it was a short note:

Dear Justin,

By the time you read this, I will be back in Cairo, and Father and I will be preparing to leave Egypt. I hope you will understand. I can't begin to tell you how much your friendship has meant to me. Thank you for your help and for your trust in me.

When I return again, you will be gone. If you want to leave me a message, use the ibis as a clue. Please destroy this note as soon as you have read it.

I'll never forget you.

Nate

After he read the note, Justin slumped to the ground and held his head in his hands. Then he read Nate's message a second and third time. Finally he sighed and stood up. He took out a match, lit it, and then blew it out.

Once again he read the note.

At last, he lit another match and touched it to the corner of the note. He held the burning piece of paper until it singed his fingers, and then he hastily dropped it. He watched until the paper was nothing but black ashes, which he ground into the desert sand.

Justin looked up to see the first tourists of the day arriving at the Temple of Abu Simbel. If he hurried, he could get a ride on their bus back to the airport.

EPILOGUE

THE NEW YORK TIMES   Wednesday, July 2, 1980

ABU SIMBEL, EGYPT—Today, Justin Sanders, age 16, led a group of archeologists and reporters through an underwater passage to a tomb that experts are already calling one of the greatest finds of the century.

Unlike King Tut's tomb, which was filled with treasure, this tomb contained only an empty alabaster chest and the unmummified skeleton of a man. Egyptologists believe the skeleton is that of Aye, a powerful advisor to the pharaohs of the 18th Dynasty, including Tutankhamon. The walls of the tomb are covered with hieroglyphic writing that appears to give a complete history of that time period.

Sanders, an American vacationing in Egypt with his parents, claims to have stumbled accidentally on the small opening leading to the cavern while scuba diving in Lake Nasser.
(continued on page 12)

Mr. Sanders put down the worn newspaper clipping and studied the top of Justin's head, which he could see above the plane seat in front of him. They were on their way back to Saudi Arabia, after delaying their departure several times because of the commotion caused by Justin's discovery at Abu Simbel.

Mr. Sanders shook his head as he considered the odd circumstances that had thrust his son into international prominence. A lucky swim, and all of a sudden, his name is immortalized—just like Howard Carter's was when Tutankhamon's tomb was discovered.

He sighed and murmured to himself, "Who would have believed it."

"What's that, dear?" Miriam asked.

"Nothing important. I was just thinking of the past few weeks. I'm finding it hard to adjust to having a celebrity for a son."

"Isn't it wonderful!" Miriam smiled. "I'm so proud of Justin."

"Well, of course! So am I. Only I'm puzzled too. I still don't understand why we couldn't say anything to the authorities about Nate and his father. I'm almost sorry that we promised Justin to keep quiet about their being involved. I wouldn't be surprised if that Alistant was some kind of international crook or spy."

"Oh, Jud, be serious. Mr. Alistant was a very wealthy man, and he just didn't want that kind of publicity—period!"

"I don't know, Miriam. I'm not convinced. One thing I am sure of, and it's that Nate wouldn't have minded the publicity."

"I agree," his wife replied. "And there's something else. I think Justin was terribly hurt by Nate's leaving so suddenly."

"He'll get over it." Mr. Sanders chuckled as he said, "Merit Bronson helped fill the void those last days in Cairo. She and Justin really hit it off."

In the seat ahead of his parents, Justin was pretending to be asleep. Head back, eyes closed, he listened to the murmur of their voices while he went over in his mind all the things that had happened during the past weeks.

It had been a hassle getting back to Cairo from Abu Simbel. The tent and all that scuba equipment made it extremely difficult to travel all by himself. And then, at the hotel, the letter from Nate's father telling him to contact Abdul Hammad at the Cairo newspaper...

After that, everything had been taken out of his hands. He was swept along on the tidal wave of publicity while his bewildered parents looked on. Justin kept wishing that Nate were there to share it all with him. He couldn't get over the feeling that his friend had betrayed him. And yet...he did understand. Nate and his father couldn't have taken the publicity. He wondered if they had returned to the space ship yet. Nate had said next month, but under the circumstances, maybe they'd already left.

No. He didn't feel betrayed that Nate had left—he was only sorry that he'd left so abruptly. He still had a thousand questions to ask. When he had fallen asleep that night at Abu Simbel, he had believed that Nate would have time to tell him all about Atlantis—exactly where the continent had been located and how it had been destroyed. And about the space ship and the experience of being in outer space. And the girl selected by the computer for Nate—what was she like?

She couldn't be any nicer than Merit, Justin thought. He and Merit had become good friends during these last weeks. She had come to the airport this morning to see him off, and they planned to write each other. Justin hoped to see her when he and his family returned to the States in September. Who knows? They might even end up going to the same university.

Thinking about the university made Justin think about his plans for the future. He had decided to major in archaeology—underwater archaeology. His father would be pleased about that. It would take time and hard work, but eventually he would become a professional archaeologist.

And someday—someday—he would find the lost continent of Atlantis!

Chronology of Ancient Egyptian History

Period	Important Events
EARLY DYNASTIC PERIOD 3100-2686 B.C. 1st and 2nd Dynasties	Capital established at Memphis by Menes, first pharaoh
OLD KINGDOM 2686-2181 B.C. 3rd-6th Dynasties	Reigns of Zoser, Cheops, Chephron. Building of the pyramids and the Sphinx.
FIRST INTERMEDIATE PERIOD 2181-2040 B.C. 7th-10th Dynasties	Period of social and political confusion
MIDDLE KINGDOM 2133-1786 B.C. 11th and 12th Dynasties	Thebes established as capital. Unification of Upper and Lower Egypt.
SECOND INTERMEDIATE PERIOD 1786-1567 B.C. 13th-17th Dynasties	Invasion and seizure of power by Asian people known as the Hyksos
NEW KINGDOM 1567-1085 B.C.	
18th Dynasty, 1567-1320 B.C.	Reigns of Akhenaton, Tutankhamon, Aye (See list of 18th Dynasty pharaohs)
19th Dynasty, 1320-1200 B.C.	Building of Temple of Abu Simbel, expansion of Temple of Karnak during reign of Ramses II, 1290-1224
20th Dynasty, 1200-1085 B.C.	Reigns of Ramses III-XI
LATE DYNASTIC PERIOD 1085-341 B.C. 21st-30th Dynasties	Period of decline and invasion by foreign powers
PTOLEMAIC PERIOD 332-330 B.C.	Alexander the Great conquers Egypt. Dynasty of Greek rulers established.

Pharaohs of the Eighteenth Dynasty

Dates of Reigns

Ahmose (AH-moz) — 1570-1546 B.C.

Amenhotep I (ah-mehn-HO-tep) — 1546-1526 B.C.

Thutmose I (THUHT-moz) — 1525-1512 B.C.

Thutmose II — 1512-1504 B.C.

Hatshepsut (haht-SHEP-soot) — 1504-1482 B.C.
Hatshepsut was regent for her stepson, the young Thutmose III, but she took the kingship for herself and ruled Egypt until her death.

Thutmose III — 1504-1450 B.C.

Amenhotep II — 1450-1425 B.C.

Thutmose IV — 1425-1417 B.C.

Amenhotep III — 1417-1379 B.C.

Amenhotep IV—Akhenaton (ak-huh-NAH-tuhn) — 1379-1362 B.C.

Smenkhare (smehn-KHAR-uh) — 1364-1361 B.C.
Smenkhare, like Tutankhamon, was a young half-brother of Akhenaton. He apparently served as co-regent with Akhenaton for two years and died very soon after him.

Tutankhamon (toot-ahngk-AH-mun) — 1361-1352 B.C.

Aye (EYE) — 1352-1348 B.C.

Horemheb (HO-rehm-hehb) — 1348-1320 B.C.
An army general who seized the throne, Horemheb was the last pharaoh of the Eighteenth Dynasty.

A Note about This Book

The story of Atlantis first appeared in the writings of Plato, who described a great island empire that sank into the Atlantic Ocean in ancient times. Since Plato's day, many people have been intrigued by the Atlantis legend, and Leona Ellerby counts herself among them. This fascination, combined with her interest in ancient and modern Egypt, inspired her first novel, *King Tut's Game Board*. A high school librarian from Oregon, Illinois, Ms. Ellerby spent several weeks in Egypt researching her book. Those parts of the story that deal with historical characters and events are factual, although the author has taken the liberty of adding an ibis to the images found on the beautiful game board from Tutankhamon's tomb. Imhotep and Aye were, of course, real people who played influential roles in Egyptian history. Presented here as visitors from Atlantis, they are characters in a story that combines fantasy and fact to provide a new version of an old legend and a glimpse of the remarkable civilization of ancient Egypt.

		DATE DUE	